# Stories by M.T. Bass

# THE INVISIBLE MIND

## MURDER BY MUNCHAUSEN BOOK #3

### BY

### M.T. BASS

AN ELECTRON ALLEY PUBLICATION

MUDCAT FALLS, U.S.A.

Electron Alley Corporation
The Herald Building
732 Broadway Avenue
Lorain, OH  44052







Manufactured in the United States of America

Edited by Elizabeth N. Love (www.bee-edited.com)

ISBN 978-1-946266-06-4 (Trade Paperback)
ISBN 978-1-946266-05-7 (eBook)

www.MTBass.net

# The Three Laws

1. A civilian-owned and operated synthetic humanoid entity may not act in any manner so as to engage in or cause any harmful or offensive contact against a human being or, through inaction, allow a human being to come to harm.

2. A civilian-owned and operated synthetic humanoid entity must obey the directives and orders given it by human beings except in those instances where such directives and orders would conflict with the First Law.

3. A civilian-owned and operated synthetic humanoid entity may protect its own existence as long as such protection does not conflict with the First or Second Laws.

Federal Technology Administration Regulations

"...he intends only his own gain, and he is in this, as in many other cases, led by an invisible hand to promote an end which was no part of his intention."

~Adam Smith, 1776

"When wireless is perfectly applied the whole earth will be converted into a huge brain, which in fact it is, all things being particles of a real and rhythmic whole."

~Nikola Tesla, 1926

"...so, too, the psyche possesses a common substratum transcending all differences in culture and consciousness. I have called this substratum the collective unconscious."

~Carl Jung, 1931

# The Baron

He savored the cruel irony of it all as he watched through the observation window in the Intensive Care Unit: Jake, the synthoid hunter, was being kept alive by machines.

Jamal, dressed in green surgical scrubs, pulled his phone out and tapped on the screen. Waitress Amy's head jerked around to the bed next to Jake's as the alarms on that patient's medical monitoring equipment began to flash and bleat.

"Code Blue to ICU bed nine," an emotionless automated voice announced over the public-address system. Soon after nurses and doctors swarmed the bed.

Jamal did not wait to watch the patient die.

In his glass-walled office in Exit Alley, one of the three cell phones neatly lined up on the credenza behind his desk dinged out Morse Code for the letter 'V', causing him to look away from the lines of computer programming language filling his laptop screen. He pulled a fourth burner phone from his shirt pocket and called the IT department at MetroHealth Medical Center, then called EC with his police issued *iPhone*.

"Just now. In bed nine, next to Jake." Q listened, then hung up.

Maddie looked around Cutty's Deli as EC, sitting across from her at a back booth, took a call. It was one of the few places where she felt safe anymore. To her, it was like home—her childhood home—warm with fond memories: of lunching with her dad once a week ever since she was twelve years old; of "Uncle" Cutty's career counseling that tipped the scales in her decision to go to the police academy instead of law school—an act of defiance to her father's urgings, but one that warmed his heart nonetheless; of endless debates on so many arcane subjects with Jake over coffee when they were partners in Robbery/Homicide. She knew it was a false sense of security; nevertheless, Maddie felt safe at Cutty's.

"That was Q," EC said, setting his phone down on the table. "He's been monitoring the data traffic in ICU. There was an inbound spike, and the patient next to Jake died."

"The Baron? Is he there?"

"Even if he was, I doubt he stuck around." EC sighed. "We should probably check it out, though."

"In a minute. Okay?" Maddie fingered the rim of her nearly empty coffee mug. "Let me, ah, finish my coffee."

"No hurry." EC wanted to say more but couldn't find the words.


Shackled to the metal bed frame, a child sat stoically staring at the door, almost as hungry for freedom as she was for food. Amy hoped someone missed her, but doubted it—after all, she was homeless and had no real family. Even if anyone did miss her, who of them would come to her rescue? Her social worker? That thought brought a wry smile to her young face. Maybe the female detective…


Though medically shackled to his hospital bed by a chemically induced coma, Jake's mind floated freely through his own subconscious, like a Freudian derelict riding the waves of swelling and ebbing dreams and memories. He was aware of waitress Amy's presence there beside him and commotion at the next bed over and even, vaguely, briefly of some malevolent presence nearby, but Jake seemed to stir or blink only when Maddie came to visit.

***~~~***

# Richard Speck

It sat on a bench outside the dormitory of nursing students, waiting with its kind's infinite patience. Originally acquired and programmed for landscaping at the Cleveland Clinic, the synthoid was one of a brigade of units which had been hacked and Munchausened, then returned to their menial daily services to mankind to await the Baron's call.

There was no adrenalin surge behind the extremely life-like facade of humanity when that call came. Data packets, sent scatter-shot through the Atlas Grid, coalesced at the location outside the Cole Eye Institute where the synthoid methodically trimmed and shaped the immaculate shrubbery around the building. To avoid Q's metadata sniffing algorithms from detecting a download spike in the grid, the information came in digital sprinkles over the course of its human handler's work shift, slowly building a malevolent intent to be executed that night. In the middle of the afternoon, the synthoid left the unfinished topiary to melt into the hospital shift change and disappeared.

Personality modules were a Gen-3 feature upgrade, which is why the earlier models were initially preferred. Swapping out a few IC chips and uploading hacked firmware was a relatively easy way to turn a quick buck with an automated contract killing. But evil innovates, too, and the same features that made synthoids even more human-like in their behavior also helped create robotic assassins which could better camouflage their malicious intents and evade the reach of the Artificial Crimes Unit by melting into and moving undetected through the humanity that surrounded them. For the Baron, it allowed for a greater measure of artistic expression in programming the synthoid's behavior to not only recreate infamous crimes of the past but to mimic the behavior of their perpetrators, which intensified the thrill of watching the video feed through the eyes of Jack the Ripper, Ted Bundy or, this particular evening, Richard Speck. Jake wasn't the only history buff, and it amused Jamal that London police had photographed the eyes of Jack the Ripper's victims, hoping to capture the last thing they ever saw: their killer's face. *If only Scotland Yard could have imagined the future.*

The Gen-3 personality modules also supported the ANSI Adaptive Artificial Intelligence Protocol #9 to enhance the artificial human experience of real men and women who interacted with synthoids. The constant writing and rewriting of code in the personality/experience loop formed unique individual synthoid consciousnesses, which manufacturers uploaded to their servers for product improvement teams to study. In Munchausened units, that feed was hijacked and routed to another portal in the Darknet to build a collective id of evil.

At eleven PM, it rose from the bench and entered the dormitory. The bodies of nine women would be found the next day, having been strangled and stabbed to death. Unlike 1966, no eyewitness was left alive, though the phrase "Born to Raise Hell" was written on the wall in blood.

***~~~***

# Slaughterhouse Five

While EC interviewed the ICU staff about the death in bed nine, Maddie sat beside Jake and read to him. EC was visibly uncomfortable whenever they came to visit. His wife never came out of her coma after the car accident just a year ago. Maddie understood how the replay with his ACU—Artificial Crimes Unit—partner bore down hard on him. She knew what he was afraid of. She feared it, too. But during her visits, the muted expressions that passed across Jake's face like a light breeze etched upon the surface of a calm pond gave her hope, and she clung desperately to it.

When they were partners and, later, lovers, Jake would teasingly give Maddie reading assignments, then quiz her relentlessly on them. Kurt Vonnegut was one of his favorite authors, so she held his hand and read him the story of Billy Pilgrim becoming unstuck in time. She knew in her heart that Jake was awake inside his lifeless body and, no doubt, bored to tears by the soap operas and game shows on the TV screens in the ward during the day for the conscious patients.

Maddie stopped in mid-sentence when she felt Jake's hand tighten around her finger. His eyes danced behind their closed lids. Maddie fearfully searched up and down the row of beds for a nurse, then felt a gentle squeeze on her finger and another. Slowly she became aware of the local news anchor interrupting

*The Days of Our Lives* on the screen up and across from Jake's bed. Nine women had been found murdered in a dormitory near University Circle. Behind the reporter at the scene, the entry to the building had been cordoned off with yellow tape and was guarded by uniformed patrolmen. Jake squeezed her hand again.

Maddie rose, kissed Jake on the forehead, then went to find EC.


"You know what Jake would want, right?" EC asked as they sat in their unmarked *Crown Vic,* watching the media jockey for camera angles and story angles among the spectators outside the yellow crime scene tape. "Eyes on the scene."

Maddie nodded. She hung her badge around her neck. "Let me go in. That way, we can keep ACU under the radar. As far as anybody knows, I'm still in Robbery/Homicide. I'll tell them Cutty asked me to check it out—worried about one of his nieces. He'll back our play."

"It won't be long before the Captain's down here."

"We've got time. He won't want to face the cameras without a full report. Besides, we've got three hours before the six o'clock news comes on." Maddie opened her car door. "Don't worry. I'm in. I'm out. Nobody gets hurt."

Once inside the crime scene tape, Maddie noticed a gray-uniformed man cut from the herd and pacing frantically. She looked back at EC and motioned him to follow her. When he caught up with Maddie, she pointed out the upset policeman, then went into the dormitory.

"Hey, son." EC held up his badge as he slowly approached the young man in his twenties. He noted the "Campus Police" patch on his sleeve.

The man spun around to face EC. His eyes darted erratically about like a caged sparrow. He wiped his mouth with his sleeve, fighting back a little spasm of dry heaves. "I-I already told the other guy everything."

"No, no. That's okay, Paul," EC said calmly, reading the name tag pinned above his shirt pocket. "It's okay."

"It was a slaughterhouse inside there. Blood everywhere. The bodies—those girls…"

"That's okay." EC slowly closed the gap between them. He put his hand on Paul's shoulder and slowly turned him away from the crime scene. He gently guided him towards the cordoned off parking lot around the side of the building, where the vans from the forensics unit and the coroner's office were parked along with several patrol cars. He spoke softly, which made Paul listen closely to hear. "We see bad things sometimes in our line of work."

Paul wiped his mouth again and nodded.

EC shook off the image of Jake's bloodied and broken body on the floor of the warehouse in the Flats. "And it's never like on a movie screen or gaming headset. It's just not."

"But those poor girls. I-I…"

"I know." EC led Paul around the back of a patrol car. They leaned against the trunk side-by-side with the dormitory behind them and looked away, towards the downtown skyline. "Did you know any of them?"

Paul shrugged. "Not really. But you see them regular like. They're familiar, you know?"

EC nodded. "How long have you been on the campus force?"

"Eighteen months. I'm finishing up my Master's in

Criminology. Hoping I can get into Quantico. But now…I don't know."

"The first one is always the hardest. You'll be fine."

"Really?"

"It doesn't get easier, but you learn to carry the weight."

"It just seems so senseless."

"How's that?"

"Why them? It was like they were picked at random."

"No recent incidents of assaults on campus?"

Paul shook his head. "He didn't even try to hide it."

"He?"

"I only saw one set of footprints between the two suites and hand prints on the hallway wall. Whoever it was didn't even try to wipe the blood off of himself."

"When did you find them?"

"It was about six-thirty or so. I was the closest one. Wish I hadn't been."

EC nodded.

They silently studied the skyline.

On the fifth floor, Maddie found the lead detective inside one of the dormitory suites, hovering over the medical examiner tech checking the liver temperature of one of the victims. She grabbed a pair of blue, disposable booties from a Bunny Suit Boy, donned them, and went into the dorm room.

"I'm going to have to get more probes," the tech from the Medical Examiner's office said. "Too many bodies."

"Do it then, *damn it.*"

Maddie did not recognize the detective. She knew all the grizzled veterans, the ones who were around when her father was still on the force. This guy was young—Maddie's age—and new to plain clothes as his suit was too fresh off the rack to have weathered many crime scenes.

He turned and ran his dark, cold, reptile-like eyes over Maddie. The tension on his face relaxed. He reflexively groomed himself by running his hand through his black, combed-back hair and checking his tie.

"I'm Maddie." She fingered the gold shield hanging at her chest. She smiled coyly.

"Derek." Her badge held his gaze, then he looked up and smiled back.

"I'm from Downtown Services—"

His smile evaporated. "Oh, great. Corporate is big-footing me already?"

"No. No. I'm here for a friend. Cutty asked me to check out the vics."

"Deli-man Cutty?"

"Yeah. He's got a niece in nursing school."

Derek relaxed again and his smile returned. He stepped up close to Maddie and scrutinized her face. "I know you, right? I never forget a redhead. The academy? No, TV. You were lead on that serial killer case, right?"

Maddie fought back a familiar wince, a reflex response whenever anyone mentioned her biggest case and, though it was not yet public knowledge, her biggest professional failure—the one that landed her in ACU. She nodded her head.

"I thought that was solved."

"Like I said. I'm just here as a favor for Cutty. What have you got?"

Derek took a step back. "What you see is what you get. A

slaughter factory. Nine all together. Four from this suite and five more from across the hall." He walked Maddie through the crime scene, carefully circumnavigating bodies and bloodstains. "We've got four out here in the living room area."

Maddie carefully eyed the victims. Three sprawled on the floor, one half-naked. The fourth sat upright on the sofa facing the dark TV screen with duct tape across her mouth and around her wrists and ankles. A huge red bib covered her chest and abdomen from a slash in the throat. "Born to Raise Hell" was written in blood on the wall over her head.

"There's two in this bedroom. One's still tucked into bed. She's probably the first." Derek looked through the doorway on the right, then stepped back for Maddie to lean in and view the student bedroom furnished with matching twin beds, dressers, and desks. A pair of MacBooks gave the room an eerie glow. "And there's three more over in this bedroom."

They walked across the living room to the other bedroom in the suite.

Maddie looked in. The room was still being photographed. "I only see two."

"One is stuffed under the bed. Weird."

They stepped back into the living room. Maddie's eyes were drawn back to the student with the slit throat watching TV. "Have you got IDs?"

"Got this list from the university." Derek offered up a piece of paper. "Of course, we'll have to verify it."

Maddie took the list, scanned it, then gave it back. "I don't see Cutty's niece."

"Good."

"Born to raise hell," Maddie read the bloody graffiti again.

Although red streams ran down the wall like excess wet paint, the handwriting caught her eye. It was too neat, too…mechanical. "What do you suppose that means?"

"Kind of obvious, don't you think?"

"Yeah, well…" Maddie took a breath. "Were any sexually assaulted?"

"Looks like it. Panties torn off three of them."

"DNA?"

"Nothing blatant. But there's tons of blood. And he might have been a…you know, non-performer. We'll have to wait for the autopsy reports."

"Just one guy?"

Derek looked around. "There's just one set of size twelve bloody footprints leading out of the apartment and down the hall."

"Just one for nine girls."

"He must have been one bad ass dude."

"No witnesses, I presume."

Derek shook his head.

"Surveillance footage coming in or out?"

"Should have been, but no such luck."

Maddie nodded as she surveyed the scene again, trying to burn every detail into her mind for Jake. "Thanks. Good luck."

"Anytime." Derek's eyes lingered on Maddie as she walked out of the apartment.

The Baron surveyed the same scene in his virtual reality headset, then skipped back to watch the nine murders again from the beginning, streamed through synthoid eyes and ears.

"Can I have more, *please?* I'm still hungry."

Jamal did not hear Amy's plea from the bedroom as the sobbing, pleading, and dying of young women filled his headset.

Outside the Cole Eye Institute, the Munchausened AnSub—Android Subject—trimmed shrubbery. Its Dermaloy skin, impervious to bleach, was blood free. Its internal silicon was also scrubbed free of malignant code and dynamic link libraries. And, of course, the last twenty-four hours of the on-board data and location recorders had been replaced with its normal daily routine.

# Exit Alley

EC waved his badge over the blinking pad to unlock the door to the Artificial Crimes Unit offices, which were down an alley and apart from the downtown district police station in a separate building. Cops in the House called it "Exit Alley" due to its reputation of being a dumping grounds for incompetents and mavericks, a last stop on the way out the door to retirement or a new career outside law enforcement. EC had requested a transfer from Robbery/Homicide after his wife's death. He mistakenly thought that chasing robots would be less stressful for a change. Jake fell into the maverick category.

Maddie hesitated as EC held the door open for her. Like EC, she had "volunteered" but, really, had no choice. Accepting the temporary assignment was the only way to clean up the mess her career had become after it turned out the perp in her series of prostitute killings in the Flats was really Jamal, recreating Jack the Ripper's crimes with Munchausened droids—and not the homeless man she had arrested and convicted to much media acclaim. And, of course, she had to do it for Jake.

"Come on, Maddie. You'll get used to it."

She shook her head. "I'm going back to Robbery/Homicide after we get him." She waved her badge over the pad and the embedded near-field communications chip logged her in. She went inside.

EC nodded, then followed her into Exit Alley.

Four rows of partitioned desks lined opposite walls of the bullpen for the detectives. The room was quiet and lifeless, like any regular office after 5 PM. Maddie's eyes gravitated to Jake's desk, which he hated with a passion—he called it a "cubicle-let," because it looked like a partitioned office cubicle that got shrunk in the wash. It was still exactly as he had left it his last day on duty, a rubbish heap of papers, food wrappers, and to-go coffee cups, a stark contrast to EC's orderly desktop beside it.

Maddie went to the far end of the bull pen where she had commandeered a small conference table for her temporary workspace. She called the Middleburg Heights PD and asked for Missing Persons to check on Amy, the missing homeless child. While waiting, she watched Samantha from the Tech Group on the other side of the building interrupt EC's concentration as he stared at his computer screen. Maddie noted that since Samantha and EC had begun dating, her appearance had become markedly less androgynous with a new, more stylish haircut, some subtle makeup and a bit more feminine cut to her wardrobe. Their involvement was one of the worst kept secrets in the building, but a subject that was never broached on duty due to department policy.

"No. Nothing yet," the Middleburg Heights detective said when he came on the line. "You know how it is. Without parents calling and constantly posting emotional pleas for their kid's return, it doesn't get much media play and fades into the pile of runaway reports. I'm sorry."

"I know. I know."

"The case is still open. I'll call if something comes up."

"Thanks." Maddie hung up and briefly considered calling the child's social worker but decided it would be a pointless exercise.

"Q's looking for us," EC said as he walked up to Maddie's table.

She nodded, and they followed Samantha to the other side of the building where the cubicle farm for the analysts and programmers was located. Q waved them into his glass-fronted corner office. He pointed at Samantha and motioned for her to join them.

Q's office furnishings were very modern, almost abstract, mainly black metal framing and glass-topped furniture. Maddie and EC sat down in webbed chairs. Everything was polished clean to the point of sterility. Severe white walls held a few colorful art prints, a Mondrian and Warhol's "Marilyn Mcnroe." The only personal picture sat on the credenza behind his desk, one of Q padded up and helmeted on a BMX bike. A skateboard leaned against the corner. It was an on-going source of speculation how someone not yet thirty had come to head the ACU tech group. The theory that nepotism was involved was partially true, though no family ties were ever identified or revealed by Q. It was also true his job was part community service arranged to atone for a youthful streak of hacking corporate IT departments, which made him imminently qualified to chase criminal hackers.

"This guy, the Baron—what's his name—Quick? Jamal?" Q asked, looking at Samantha. He tapped nervously on his glass desktop with the pad of his index finger.

"E.J. Quick is an online persona for his blog and tech reporting." Samantha hesitated and looked at Maddie. "Jake called him Jamal, but there's nothing that comes up in data searches that makes any connections."

"Whoever he is—if he's really the Baron—this guy is damn good." The rhythm of Q's tapping increased. "We're still deconstructing the code we seized at the warehouse. It's intense."

"The invisible—" Maddie started to say.

Q's hand froze in mid-tap, and he quickly cut her off. "I'm not ready to, ah, publicly advance that theory."

Maddie frowned at Q.

He slowly shook his head and scanned around the room with his eyes while tugging his ear.

EC looked from Maddie to Q, then back to Maddie. Jake was the only one who ever seemed to connect with Q in a way that went beyond the departmental roles spelled out in official job descriptions. EC took note that Maddie seemed to have filled that void but didn't press. He'd find out soon enough, just like with Jake. EC preferred not expending his patience on stroking—or teasing—*prima donnas.*

"What about physical evidence from the warehouse?" Q turned and asked EC.

"There were a dozen synthoids in the place in various stages of teardown and rebuild."

"A serious chop-shop?"

"Definitely a production line operation. Bob and Puff are working through the ones we took into evidence. Not much there." EC shook his head. "No telling how many they had run through there and released back into the wild, but it almost looks like they were trying to create their own little army or something."

"And we haven't gotten anything from the warm bodies we rounded up." Maddie sighed. "The homeless camped out on the first floor were truly clueless, and the hackers upstairs have all lawyered up with some high-priced downtown suits."

"Who's paying for that?" Q asked.

"Good question. They all made bail, too."

"County auditor's records show the building was owned free and clear by an LLC called White Chapel, which, of course, was also Jack the Ripper's London stomping grounds," EC said. "Without a mortgage, though, we're going to have to pull tax and utility records to dig up some banking records. McGinty's office is working on the subpoenas."

"What about corporate records?"

"The incorporation papers list a rogue's gallery of serial killers for the company officers: Henry Lee Lucas, Albert DeSalvo, Ed Gein, John Gacy."

"Where's the corporate offices?" Q asked.

"The East Ninth Street address on file is about three blocks into Lake Erie," Maddie answered.

"So, what now?"

EC looked around the room and pulled his *iNode* off his belt and put in on Q's desk.

Q nodded and put his *AlphaBit* on the desk. He looked at Samantha and shook his head.

Maddie anted up her *iNode* and the three of them went down the hall and out an emergency exit into the alley. Q went through the motions of disabling the security camera with a burner phone.

"You heard about the murders in University Circle?" Maddie asked.

Q nodded. "The Baron?"

"We think so. We're just trying to figure out the copycat

connection. The only thing we've got is that 'Born to Raise Hell' was written on the wall in blood."

"And all I've come up with on that so far are links to a heavy metal song and a two-star Steven Seagal movie from decades ago," EC said. "Take a look at the case file and run the MO through your magic algorithm for a match up."

"Can do." Q scratched the back of his head. "Under the radar, right?"

"We're not out here in the alley for the ambiance." EC looked at Maddie. "A real wizard of smart, eh?"

Q scowled and went back into the ACU offices.

"What do you think?" EC asked Maddie as they followed Q into the building. "Want to get some carry-out from King Wah's?"

"You know, it's been a long day," Maddie said wearily. "And I think I need to put some distance between me and that bloody dorm room scene."

"Sure. Understood."

"I'll take a stack of documents home and go through them later."

Maddie and EC retrieved their *iNodes* from Q's empty office. Then Maddie went home, and EC went in search of Samantha.

***~~~***

## So It Goes...

Maddie woke at four-thirty the next morning. The file folders, pictures, and documents seized in the warehouse raid were still stacked neatly on the breakfast bar of her condo where she put them the night before. An empty wine glass was parked next to the kitchen sink. She avoided eye contact with the pile of evidence as she passed by on the way to the refrigerator to pour a glass of orange juice, gulping it down as she walked back to her bedroom to get dressed in running shorts, Nikes, and a gray F.B.I. Quantico hoody. On the way out the door, she grabbed her Glock 26 off-duty pistol and put it into the fanny pack around her waist with her keys.

Crocker Park was still a suburban petri dish of shops, apartments, restaurants, cluster homes, and businesses, all artfully arranged by architects to mimic that damn Bedford Falls in the movie Jake used to make her watch every Christmas, *It's a Wonderful Life*—in black-and-white no less. But, it was easy. You could buy your way into a cozy small-town, Mayberry-like existence with mere mortgage approval from the bank. She eventually learned to ignore Jake's teasing.

The streets were still dark and deserted when Maddie started her run. She liked that she could serpentine through the streets without having to jink and zig-zag around pedestrians and traffic. The slap of her running shoes echoed softly down the canyons of glass storefronts until she got to the greenbelt where commerce stopped and the Metroparks started. She steeled herself to continue on the trail through the woods. It still took some effort to venture forth alone, even in familiar places, after being ambushed and assaulted by the synthoid down in the Flats. By the time she got back, Sysco food and Orlando bakery trucks were making their early morning deliveries to the restaurants; the smell of fresh brewed coffee wafted from Starbucks, bagel shops, and bakeries; and the early-rising corporate ladder-climbers marched zombie-like towards their offices.

Maddie skipped her usual post-run dark roast and scone to shower, dress, and get on the road so she could stop by the old Glick Building Jake owned on Detroit Avenue which used to be his parents' flower shop. He lived in the second-floor apartment and turned the storefront downstairs into a huge mancave in the front and a workshop garage in the back. She knew Jake would have never given waitress Amy a key to his place, so Maddie had been checking his mail and tending to Frank the Feral Cat—if he was around. Sometimes it was not clear whether Jake adopted Frank or vice versa.

Maddie lingered upstairs, wandering from room to room, remembering better times. She grabbed Jake's hardback copy of *Huckleberry Finn* off the bookshelf in his living room, then drove to MetroHealth Medical Center, passing by John's Diner down the street to make sure that waitress Amy's car was in the lot.

A swell of hot panic crested in Maddie's neck when she got to the ICU and found Jake's bed empty.

"He came around late yesterday," Kindra, one of the R.N.s who had taken care of Jake, smiled and said as Maddie approached the nurse's station. "Isn't it great? They transferred him upstairs just a bit ago. He's in room seven-thirty-four."

Upstairs, Maddie hung back in the hallway and watched Jake leisurely savor cubes of red Jell-O. She smiled. He still had his typical, tousled morning hair after waking up from the coma. Though his face was scruffy, thin, and a bit haggard from the lack of real food, his blue eyes were clear and sharp, intently staring a hole into the wall across from his bed as he ate.

Maddie took a deep breath, exhaled slowly, then entered the room. "I thought you hated that stuff."

"I hate hospitals, too, but here I am." Jake slurped another Jell-O cube and smiled. He winked at Maddie. "So it goes…"

He *knew*. Maddie felt tears roll down her cheeks. "You heard me?"

"Vonnegut is always a good choice."

She quickly wiped her cheek. Stepping next to the bed, she took Jake's hand and squeezed tightly. She smiled broadly. "Uh, yeah, but…you know, Jell-O?"

"Oh, it hurts going down from the tubes. But at the same time feels good. Kind of like life."

"We'll have to get a real, home-cooked meal in you." She kissed the back of his hand. Their personal relationship began after she consoled Jake with food when their professional relationship ended with his suspension—until their personal relationship ended when Jake used Maddie for Munchausen bait in the Flats that got her attacked by the synthoid.

"Just promise me, no Jell-O."

"No Jell-O. I promise." She smiled and shook her head. "EC will be glad to hear you're vertical again."

"How's he doing?"

"Good. We're, ah, kind of working together."

"Don't tell me you got booted to ACU."

"I volunteered…sort of. Kind of had to do it to clean up the mess with the Steinmauer case."

"Not permanent, though. Right?" Jake asked.

"Sands assured me I could go back to Robbery/Homicide."

"I don't know. You might get hooked on it."

"Doubtful. Very doubtful."

Jake looked away and stared off into space. He had no choice when he got sent to Exit Alley. It was either take the transfer or lose his job. You can't shoot and kill a Councilman's son without consequences. He sighed and asked, "What's going on with the murder of those nurses? Not much on the news."

"A District Three guy named Derek caught the case. I think he's new in plain clothes."

"Not ACU?"

"The Baron's not really public knowledge…so far. Sands wants to keep it that way until we make up some ground on him."

"And Jamal?"

"In the wind."

"He did it," Jake said. "He did those nurses. You know that."

Maddie nodded her head. "But we can't figure out the angle. EC and I went down there and checked out the scene. Bad, bloody bad. 'Born to Raise Hell' was written on the wall in it. But, the handwriting—too, ah, font-like, if you know what I mean."

"Born to raise hell? That was Richard Speck. He stabbed and strangled eight nursing students back in the Sixties."

"Yeah? But we've got nine vics."

Jake thought for a moment. "Was one of the bodies stuffed under a bed?"

Maddie nodded.

"Yeah…right."

"What?"

"It is Speck. That *son-of-a-bitch.*"

"What? Jamal?"

"Uh-huh. The Chicago cops caught Speck because a ninth student hid under a bed. She watched him kill the others and saw a tattoo on his arm."

"What was it?"

Jake gave Maddie an impatient look.

*"Born to raise hell."*

Jake nodded. "That's how they found him. From the eyewitness who survived. So, the Baron wasn't just doing another copycat. He's fixing history."

Maddie shook her head.

"I've got to get out of here."

"No. You can't."

"I know Jamal. I can stop him." Jake started to get up.

Maddie pushed him back down into bed. "But not if you check out AMA, before you've regained your strength. You'll just crash again."

"But I can help."

"I know. I know."

Jake pushed back against Maddie, but she held him down, too easily.

"I've got half a stack of evidence from the warehouse raid in my car. I'll sign it over to you and get the other half from EC."

Jake eased back into the bed.

"I'm not even sure what I should be looking for, so go through it while you recoup. Rest and get your body right. When the docs green-light you, come help us."

Jake nodded.

"And I'll make that home-cooked meal I promised. Chicken Parm sound good?"

Jake smiled. "Deal."


Jamal stood by the "Please Seat Yourself" sign next to the cash register at John's Diner and watched the choreography of the waitresses serving the tail end of the breakfast rush. When she went back into the kitchen, he took an empty booth in waitress Amy's section and perused a menu.

"Hey…you're Jake's reporter buddy, right?" Amy asked, sliding onto the bench across from Jamal.

He lowered the menu and smiled. "And you are Amy, correct? Jake's a lucky guy. A very lucky guy."

Amy lowered her eyes and smiled, tucking an errant strand of blonde hair back behind her ear.

Jamal stared hungrily.

"Have you decided, yet?"

"Mmmm…not exactly."

"Coffee, then?"

"Sure."


**~~~***

# The Black Tier

Nothing Q ever saw in cyberspace scared him, until now. Behind the depravity found in the Darknet, it was still intensely logical, because, after all, that's what programming is: logic. And that made it understandable intellectually, emotionally disengageable and, therefore, at least somewhat manageable ethically. At least that was what he always told himself.

In the dead of night, Q sat on the second floor of the warehouse in the Flats admiring and fearing the racks of servers humming, blinking, and internally generating malignant code on its own. While he was safe from outside intruders by the patrol unit parked out front guarding the building downstairs, Q was vulnerable to the illogic of the Baron's evil inhabiting the millions of silicon circuits surrounding him.

He had not been completely forthcoming with Maddie, EC, and Lt. Sands in telling them the server farm was "air-gapped"—completely cut off from the outside world with no physical or wireless connections to any other network. He could have done it that way, but to stop the Baron's experiment would mean sacrificing crucial evidence…and leaving his own curiosity unsatisfied—a curiosity that often led him into trouble. Now, though, he had a bigger problem. His tracking algorithms had not caught the metadata push through the Atlas Grid into the AnSub like before; but, here, Q had observed the inbound "eyes and ears" feed from the Speck copycat murders at the University Circle dormitory in real time. The video was disturbing enough, but the flurry of encrypted I/O activity in a "black" tier of the data center he had not yet been able to penetrate haunted him.

Jake was right: true horror is not in eye of the beholder but in his imagination. And while Jake was a techno-fossil, his instincts were like something out of Harry Potter. The detective could also read people like they were billboards, which made him a somewhat dangerous ally for Q—but an ally he wished at that moment was there to help him.

Q got up and turned off the overhead florescent lights. The room took on an eerie neon glow of blue and green from the cabinet lights, annunciator panels, and monitor screens. He wandered up and down the rows of eight-foot tall racks filled with server blades, RAID storage drive modules, and patch bays sprouting Cat5e cables like ivy vines entwining themselves on the sacred halls of learning at the colleges he had been expelled from. He could feel his skin moisten with sweat from the heat thrown off by the electronics. A musty hint of ozone floated in the air.

Q stopped at a shelf sticking out with a keyboard and monitor in a row deep inside the Baron's server farm. He split the screen into two windows, one to monitor the traffic activity into and out of the impenetrable Black Tier. In the other window, he called up the synthoid's video stream of the brutal slayings of the nine student nurses. As it played, the graphs and data streams spiked and ebbed with each killing and stalking. He played the video again, this time monitoring his own reactions as he forced himself not to look away—revulsion at the slashing, choking brutality; ratcheting dread of anticipation; bottomless sorrow at the broken and lifeless evidence of inhumanity as the synthoid panned at the end to survey his handiwork—Richard Speck's programmed handiwork.

Q closed his eyes. He bent over the keyboard and drew deep breaths until he felt his heart rate slow again, then turned his eyes back to the monitor screen.

As the video played again, he watched the window with the graphs and data streams, realizing that deep within the Black Tier, the machine was reacting emotionally…just as he had.

***~~~***

# Broken Dreams

Maddie slept fitfully. When she woke, vague reverberations of dread haunted her. Not knowing if it was her dreams or a premonition, she called down to MetroHealth Medical Center and checked with the nurses on the seventh floor. Jake was resting comfortably.

*Figures.* She flopped back down on her pillow and stared at the ceiling. She hated the waiting: waiting for Q to crack the computer code enigma; waiting on Jake to review the evidence collected from warehouse; waiting for the investigation of the student nurses' murders to hit a dead end; waiting for a hit on the BOLO for Jamal; waiting for one of the Baron's minions to rise and attack; waiting for Jake to get out of the hospital.

She got up and ran, and the act of running pounded away the haunting thoughts. After, Maddie mindlessly went through her morning ritual and headed downtown. Normally, she would go to her desk in Robbery/Homicide and savor a cup of coffee in the quiet before the shift change began to fill the bull pen with fellow detectives. It wasn't the same in Exit Alley where the tech analysts seemed to have no sense of time, coming and going at all hours of the day. There was never any peace and quiet there. Besides, she had no home—no desk to call her own—just temporary squatter's rights on a conference table.

So, Maddie stopped at Cutty's deli, grabbing a cup of coffee and a bagel with a smear of cream cheese. She parked herself in the back booth she and Jake shared when they were work partners where they would watch the comings and goings in the deli. But she didn't, instead staring into her coffee mug and lamely skating the bagel around on her plate like a hockey puck.

"I figured I might find you here." Derek, the detective from District Three, sat down across from her in Jake's spot.

Maddie noted his wry smile and was immediately on guard. "You're kind of off the beaten path, no?"

Derek shrugged.

Cutty suddenly appeared beside the table. He eyeballed the stranger in his place with suspicion. "Hey, Madeline. Who's your friend?"

"This is Derek. He caught the case of the nine student nurses."

"Yeah…on the news. I seen it."

"How is your niece doing?" Derek turned his head up towards Cutty but kept his eyes on Maddie.

Cutty took a long, loud slurp of scotch out of his CPD coffee mug that drew Derek's eyes. He caught the quick furrow in Maddie's brow and the jerk of her head across the table. Cutty shook his head. *"Kids.* Glad I never had any. First, they eat you out of house and home, then suck up your pension to party on for four more years. But, hey, that's my sister's problem."

Derek nodded slowly, then looked over at Maddie. He smiled knowingly.

She smiled back.

"Can I get you anything, detective?" Cutty asked.

"No, thanks. I've been called down to the Director's palace to brief the powers that be."

"Suit yourself. Good luck with the case," Cutty said as he walked away.

"Great to be in the spotlight, eh?" Derek asked Maddie.

"Depends."

"On?"

Maddie thought for a moment. "Whether it's the glow of admiration or heat for getting roasted. They weren't too kind to one of my former partners."

"The one that shot the councilman's son?"

Maddie nodded.

"Well, from what I saw online, the camera likes you—a lot." Derek studied Maddie's face as if inventorying her features and counting the few freckles splashed on her cheeks. "I'll bet you've got a lovely off-duty smile."

She turned her head down and away to hide her blushing and a reflex smile. *That's Jake's line.*

Having hit his mark, Derek slid out of the booth and stood up. "Do me a favor, will you?"

"What's that?"

"The case—my case." Derek looked over at Cutty behind the counter, then back at Maddie with a serious expression. "If you know something—if you hear anything, please let me know. Don't let me get hung out to dry. Please."

Maddie looked up. Her smile slowly drooped away. She met his eyes and nodded.

"Thanks."

As Derek walked out, he passed by EC on his way in, who turned and watched him leave the deli.

"Do I know that guy?" EC asked as he came up to Maddie.

"He's the lead on the nurse murders. I met him when we were at the crime scene."

"Oh." EC sat down where Derek had been. "Old habits die hard, huh."

Maddie frowned.

"You know—Jake. You guys used to meet here, too, right? This booth should have his name on it."

She nodded, looking at the deli door.

"Man, that guy."

"Huh?"

"Jake."

"Yeah, Jake."

"So…Samantha thinks she found something as we were going through stuff from the warehouse last night."

"Last night?"

EC looked down as he wrung his hands. "I-I—we…"

Maddie grabbed his hands. "Let's just go see what she has."

EC nodded, and they got up to leave.

On the way out, Maddie stopped and leaned over the deli counter. "Thanks, Uncle Cutty."

"My niece, huh?" Cutty paused and looked up from the brisket of corned beef he was slicing. "My brother-in-law still has tuition nightmares. Better him than me."

"Just a little cover."

Cutty eyeballed Maddie with a squint. "You guys be careful out there. It's a mean old world."

"Thanks." Maddie started to follow EC out.

"And say hi to Jake for me."

She looked back, and Cutty was working on the brisket

again. Back at Exit Alley, Maddie waited in the conference room while EC fetched Samantha. "Where's Q?" she asked when they returned.

"I guess he's still down in the Flats at the server farm," Samantha said. "He's taken that on personally and has been spending most of his time down there."

"Making any progress?"

"Don't know. He's pretty tight lipped about it."

"And what have you got?"

Samantha sat down with her *iSlate* and began swiping across its screen.

Maddie watched a moment, then looked impatiently at EC, who sat down beside Samantha.

"I've been going through the evidence from the warehouse," EC said. "There's some creepy stuff in it, but I'm not seeing much of a pattern or anything."

"I hope Jake can come up with something." Maddie shook her head. "I don't see anything that's going to help us get Jamal."

"So…I went and pulled down as many of the E.J. Quick articles as I could find off of his blog and from news sites," Samantha said, eyes still locked on the screen of her *iSlate*. "And ran them through the Strunk-Skinner meat grinder—"

"What's that?" Maddie asked.

"It's an analytical tool that evaluates grammar, vocabulary, syntax, form, structure, allusions, figures of speech, and patterns of thematic development to construct a unique linguistic fingerprint." Samantha spun the tablet around towards Maddie to show her a screen tiled with graphs, numbers, and cryptic codes.

"And, since we already have his articles, this can help us, how? After all, we can just read what he wrote, right?"

"Well, some posit the theory that it goes deeper—metaphysically and ontologically—that it represents an individual's cognitive schematic—how he perceives and processes and structures the world in his head."

"Profiling? How is that going to help? We already know who the bad guy is."

"Yeah. Kind of. But there's more to it than that."

"More? I've read his stories. It's pretty straight forward reporting for the most part."

Samantha looked at EC for help. "The next step is to take Jamal's linguistic fingerprint and start looking for it across the web…and in the Darknet."

Maddie frowned. She looked at EC, too.

"He's out there networking with others, above ground and under," EC explained. "Social media, chat rooms—who knows where else—and who knows with what identities. But he's using words, mainly—maybe some pics, but mostly words. And with the S&S profile, we can find him under whatever rocks he and his cohorts are hiding."

"And once we start matching up posts to the profile," Samantha added, "we might be able to map his trail and find him."

"Find him in cyberspace? We need to find him in the real world and stop him," Maddie insisted. "And stop him quick."

"But that's just it," Samantha said. "He has to post from somewhere in the real world. This guy is extremely careful and uses a bit scatter masking protocol, even on his E.J. Quick stories. But they're not infallible. And not everybody he interacts with may be as disciplined as he is. We look for cracks in the castle wall."

Maddie sighed. *Techno mumbo-jumbo.* She looked at a complex abstract print on the wall of the conference room. It was an extreme closeup of a microchip circuit, a labyrinth carved in silicon. There was no clear way in or out of the maze.

"I think it will help find him," Samantha said.

Maddie looked at Samantha and smiled. *Whatever…*

"What have we got to lose?" EC asked.

"I don't know. Nothing I guess," Maddie answered. *Except my sanity.*

Amy woke with a start from her dream: a grim fairy tale of a young girl trapped in a castle tower. She closed her eyes quickly, confronted with her own imprisonment. In her self-imposed darkness, she stoked her anger with thoughts of revenge.

***~~~***

# Homecoming

Jake stepped out of the Westlake Express cab in front of the Glick Building on Detroit Road carrying a plastic bag with the few possessions that came with him into the emergency room—except for his shield. Lt. Sands held his badge for safekeeping. Police evidence, discharge papers, and medication filled another bag with a matching blue-and-green MH logo. The sweat suit nurse Kindra bought for him at the Walmart by MetroHealth Medical Center aged him artificially by hanging loosely on his frame, an impression aided by his slow, shuffling gate. He couldn't wait to get into a hot shower to scrub the sick from the hospital off his skin. But when he got upstairs to his apartment, a wave of fatigue swelled over him and he sank into the sofa in his living room.

When he woke from the nap his body imposed on his mind, he was still weary. He smirked. *Must have taken more energy than I thought to convince the doctor I was good to go for discharge.*

At the door to the fire escape on the back of the building, Jake heard a familiar scratching. "Duty calls."

He got up to let Frank the Feral Cat in, twisting, stretching, and pulling his arms and legs as he went to wring the ache out of his muscles put there by the synthoid that manhandled him at the warehouse in the Flats. Frank led him back to the kitchen to be fed.

"Slim pickings, my man." Jake set down a bowl of dry cat food, which Frank sniffed, then walked away from.

Jake pulled down a box of *Cheerios* for himself. He went to the refrigerator and grabbed the gallon jug of milk, but it didn't pass the smell test, so he dumped it and tossed a handful of pulverized oats into his mouth.

"Yeah. I get it," Jake said to Frank, crunching on the dry cereal. "So, should we call for pizza or Chinese—oh, sorry about that, pal. Pizza it is."

As Jake finished texting his order to Angelo's, a knock drew their eyes towards the front door. Jake reached into the dishwasher and grabbed his Colt 1911.

"Come on in."

A moment later, Q walked into the kitchen. "Don't you think it would be a good idea to lock your door?"

"A lock is just a speed bump, not protection." Jake sat down at the kitchen table and laid the pistol in front of him. "Grab a beer."

"Jesus. You look like hell." Q opened the refrigerator and peered in. He pulled out a Shiner Bock long neck and twisted off the cap. "Are you sure you should be out yet?"

Jake grunted.

Q sat down across from Jake. "So, what's so important?"

"I want you to do something about this." Jake pulled up his left sleeve and rolled his arm palm up. He pointed to a dark shadow beneath the skin of his forearm. "This. Turn it off or spoof it or...*something.*"

"An implant for monitoring your vitals?"

"It was the only way they would release me."

"Big Doctor is watching, eh?"

"Yeah. Well, not me. 'Cause if they can, the Baron can."

"Right." Q's grin evaporated. "Get me your *iNode.*"

Jake pushed himself up from the table and went into the living room. "We're getting pizza. You in?"

"We?"

Jake pointed at Frank flopped down in the middle of the kitchen floor and slid his *iNode* across the table to Q.

"As long as there's no anchovies on it, I'm in." Q pulled out a phone and began tapping on the screen.

"Right. No anchovies." Jake watched Q work. "Have you found it yet?"

"What? This? Piece of cake. I'll patch it to a biorhythm routine in the cloud based on your medical records. By the time they figure it out, you'll be the picture of health."

"No. You know what I mean." Jake leaned in. "The server farm."

Q looked up. He nodded slowly. "I found it, but...you're not going to like it."

"Didn't think I would."

"There's a black tier in the configuration that's sucking in data, churning it, and spitting it back out. I haven't broken the encryption on the code yet, but it seems to be what they call curved logic."

"What's that?"

"Beyond straight-line *If—And—Or—Therefore* progressive machine think." Q chuckled to himself and shook his head. "Intuitional—like you."

"To what end?"

Q looked up with a serious look on his face. "I don't know."

Jake read Q's face. "Yeah. You do."

"I don't know for sure, but…" Q sighed. "It's reactionary, not just causal. You know, cause, effect—*reaction*. There's a working theory out there that AI can develop a consciousness. That it can become an invisible mind, competitive with human intellect. An unseen force that can bend the cultural evolutionary time line."

"You guys. Always have to try to rule the world."

"Yeah, but—I mean, but what if it wasn't just—wasn't strictly an intellectual force?"

"What other kind of force could there be inside the machine?"

"When I played the synthoid A/V stream of the nurse murders, there was a reaction to it—just like I reacted to it. Inside. I can't give you calibrated percentages or timeline overlays or anything, but just like my heart rate and respirations rose and fell, so did CPU usage, memory I/O, network streaming, like—like—"

"Like artificial emotions."

Q nodded.

"Great. Just what the world needs: hormonal technology." Jake gazed off into space. "I guess that explains that."

"What?"

"I've been going through the piles of physical evidence taken from the warehouse. Papers, pictures—out of the file cabinets and off the walls. There were the usual homages to Tesla, Turing, Jobs, and Musk—"

"Mount *Tech*more."

"Huh?"

"Mount Techmore. You know, there's North Dakota, South Dakota, and Geek Dakota."

Jake shook his head. "Whatever. But there were also shrines on the wall to Freud, Jung, and Skinner."

"Freud? What's that all about?"

"You know that consciousness is just one side of the coin."

"Coin?"

"Heads and tails. You've got the thinking side and the feeling side. The id. The entire history of AI has been on the ego and super ego side. Now…"

"How does that help control the world?"

"It doesn't. And maybe that's not what he wants."

"What does the Baron want?"

"Look at the personalities he is going id mining in. What do you think?"

The Angelo's delivery man arrived.

Jake, Q, and Frank ate the pizza in silence, lost in their own private thoughts.

When Maddie let herself into Jake's apartment the next morning, Frank greeted her at the door. After a perfunctory petting, he scurried out, leaving Maddie to wonder how he had gotten in. She listened to the apartment, then drew her Glock and slowly moved through the rooms. A pizza box and beer bottles were on the kitchen table. The living room was empty. Two MetroHealth Medical Center plastic bags were on the sofa. As she moved towards the bedrooms, she could hear a soft snoring. She peeked around the doorway and saw Jake sleeping in his bed. She was mad, then happy, then a bit irked. She holstered her Glock.

Maddie went into the kitchen and called EC to tell him she

would be late for work. After making a pot of coffee, she sat with Jake while he slept, reading *The Red Dragon* by Thomas Harris.

***~~~***

# Murder Keep

Sometimes, he could feel the electro-magnetic fields of high-voltage power lines literally bruising his soul. So, one of the many renovations he made to his lair was to embed a Faraday cage behind the walls, ceiling, and the sub-floor of the windowless hideaway built off the second-floor master bedroom. There were no lights or electrical outlets in the room and all the copper wires had been stripped off the studs before the insulation and walls were put up. When the pressure of radio waves, which inexorably flooded the aether ever since the time of Marconi, grew unbearable, he retreated into its darkness to seek relief from his migraines. The extensive sound-proofing added throughout the old stone structure helped as well.

Jamal emerged refreshed and parked himself in the armchair by the turret windows of the master bedroom. He watched midnight traffic trickle this way and that on Franklin Avenue and West Forty-fourth Street. He checked his watch. The download to the next Munchausened synthoid would take well into tomorrow's swing shift to complete. Then, the murder clock would start ticking down. In the empty time, he could watch replays but decided against it, preferring to let the anticipation build within himself, like a Cedar Point roller coaster ratcheting up ever higher into the sky. In truth—and

Jamal prided himself on not being self-delusional—he realized his anticipation needed amping up even more lately.

His castle was quiet. He could sleep but knew he wouldn't.

*I could eat. But why?*

He felt no physical hunger.

A patrol car drifted by slowly on Franklin Avenue. Jamal briefly wondered how Jake was doing, then lit up his *iSlate,* using its encrypted Sawtooth wireless to connect into the web of security cameras, microphones, and sensors spread both outside and throughout the inside of the house. It was the only network he allowed in the entire building. No cell phones or connected devices like *iNode*s were permitted inside. Utility smart-meters had been spoofed with digital images of "normal" household activity. Behind that facade, the residence was a dark hole on the Atlas Grid. A brief scan around the perimeter revealed no movement. The front, back, and side doorways were closed. The green lights on the control panel indicated they were safely locked. The staircases, halls, and hidden passageways were empty.

Downstairs in the basement servant's quarters, devoted caretakers Bill and Stephanie slept soundly. On the main level, Carbon, an all-black cat, sat at his perch on the table in the parlor front window, directly below, watching the street scene out front as well.

The previous owners had sacrificed one of the six bedrooms on the second floor to create a completely hidden safe room that only he, Bill and Stephanie knew about. There, Amy slept peacefully.

Jamal broke the "fifth wall," a carefully maintained cyber firebreak between him and his synthoid minions, by taking the urchin off the street and bringing her there to taunt Jake. An impulsive move questioned less now, he found it stirred something new and darker still within him to have had, physically, "hands-on" an illicit act.

As he watched Amy sleep, the Baron marveled at these feelings and wondered what new mayhem they might bring.

***~~~***

# The Au Pair

The mousy hair was cut short and styled simply with a part in the middle. A pair of softened blue-gray eyes belied a careful attentiveness to the activities on the lakeside playground where young preschoolers ran and swung and climbed and slid down timber, steel, and plastic structures designed for maximum childhood fun within the legal and bureaucratic strictures deemed necessary for public safety and risk aversion.

Feature set E-DC640827-JA-451010 Rev. C, based on an Anglo-Saxon female, was aged for twenty years, six months, and mounted on a five-foot, eight-inch, fifty-eight-kilogram chassis designed to evoke mild to low-scale moderate male attraction. The optimized occupational wardrobe set included knee-level skirts, jumpers, and loose-fitted slacks paired with cotton blouses and knit tops sleeved appropriate to the season, though ambient temperatures were rarely a functional consideration except in severe climate extremes when auxiliary heating or cooling was recommended, either with internal HVAC micro-units or with temperature-compensating outer garments.

"Julie" sat on a bench at her post near the entrance to the playground as part of a one-person, two-synthoid team to supervise the forty children of the daycare center out for afternoon recreation at the public park. Programmed for surveillance and child care assistance, she maintained a continuous scan of the activities in her sector like an air traffic controller monitoring the flow of flights into and out of a busy airport, ready to issue verbal instructions or to intervene physically if threat of harm appeared to her charges.

As a cost-cutting measure, the daycare center, like so many other businesses with a small synthoid head count, transported their units to a suburban service center for the mandated biennial inspection, rather than pay for a "house call" by a certified technician. From there, Julie's review was subcontracted to a company in a warehouse in the Flats where some special modifications were also made, including the unlocking of port 139 for remote access via the Atlas Grid.

Julie's wellness software failed to detect the snippets of malicious machine code slowly trickling into unused memory registers, piggy-backed on the routine hive monitoring traffic which would soon be ghosted to send false location and status information up to her manufacturer's customer service and tech support servers. The scattered puddles of data and malware agents would soon begin to pool, multiply, and migrate throughout the operating system, BIOS, and Biology Logic Controller modules, attaching themselves to host routines and supplanting datalink libraries. With her civilian "Three Laws" chip set critically crippled during her biennial inspection, Julie would soon be as deadly as any government "Specials Operations" synthoid.

As playtime for the children came to the end of its allotted time period, the daycare's certified human child and synthoid minder rose from her bench, shadowed by Julie and the other PSA unit. They shepherded the boys and girls together and walked them back to the nearby center. After the last parent retrieved their child at the end of the Friday work day, Julie was parked at her charging station for the weekend.

When the battery packs reached one-hundred percent shortly after two AM, Julie came out of sleep mode, assumed a new functional identity, and let herself out of the facility. As planned, she would not be discovered missing for two days. Her first task was to retrieve the pistol and ammunition cached for her back at the lakeside park.

# Overkill

Maddie sat at the ten-foot-long wood conference table Q used as a workspace in the second-floor server room of the White Chapel LLC building in the Flats. Her phone and *iSlate* were dark. In the dim lighting, she waited for Jake and EC to come back from their guided stroll through the labyrinth of eight-foot-tall racks of blinking servers. She had seen it all before. She did not need to look at it again, so she stared out the window at an ore boat crawling its way up the river, doubting it was right for Jake to be there on his first day back to work.

Hundreds of small plastic cooling fans running in the back planes of various modules in the racks pumped the room full of warm air and raised the ambient noise level with a subtle hum which Maddie noticed most by its absence when she got back outside.

*With all the hours Q spends down there, how can he not be stark raving mad himself?*

As they U-turned around the end of an aisle, Jake's eyes were drawn to Maddie by the window cooling herself by fanning her blouse over her breasts with her head tilted back and her eyes closed. Q's voice up ahead faded away in his consciousness as Jake slowed and swiveled his head to keep her in his gaze. EC noticed, but said nothing.

The walk-through over, Q and EC sat down at the conference table across from Maddie. Jake went to the window and looked at the bend in the river, now empty as the ore boat had moved upriver. The hum of the cooling fans seemed to grow louder in their silence.

"Where are they on the Speck murders?" Jake finally asked.

"I've been monitoring the murder book through a server back channel," Q said. "No eye witnesses came out of the campus canvas. Lots of ugly pictures from the crime scene and lots of blood samples, but no forensics on a perp."

"There won't be any." Jake sighed.

"Most of what's going on now is background interviews—family, friends, faculty—and scavenging social media accounts. Probably trying to find a jilted lover of one of the girls or something."

"What else can they do," EC said.

"Should we tell them?" Maddie asked.

Jake turned from the window and looked at Q. "Anything?"

"We've gone through the metadata off the traffic logs and LUDs. All the university units are accounted for and the few other synthoids active that night were on the periphery of the sector and didn't get near the dorm."

"And this place?"

"There's nothing to bloodhound back to this location or to any of the NSA portals in the grid we've staked-out," Q answered. "Sorry."

Jake sat down next to Maddie. "What do we tell them?"

Maddie shrugged and shook her head.

"What about Jamal?" EC asked.

"A phantom," Q said. "Actually, a shadow of a phantom. Samantha's been trying to track his online activity linguistically.

He's a clever fellow. His reporting is highly stylized, and she's gotten some hits, but they're all phishing and fraud cases from over a decade ago, so she'll have to take a closer look. Nothing at all in the Darknet chat rooms and social media we're monitoring. What is unusual is that some of those postings seem machine generated. They're almost generic. Pretty unusual for such fringe personalities."

"Is he using an AI composition bot to hide behind?" EC asked.

"Could be. That or there are apps that run what you've written through a series of translations—Portuguese to Mandarin to Hebrew to Russian then back to English—which scrubs out language identity markers. She's checking those posts to see if there are any hits in the headers and routing that match up. It's a long shot, since even on his signed blog posts, the guy uses a high-level Tor onion services protocol."

"Which means?" Jake asked impatiently.

"Which means the paths of his online activity get whipped, grated, and pureed through an IP blender and can't be tracked."

"Figures." EC shook his head. "Could be anywhere, then. Right?"

"That's the idea. But sometimes you get lucky."

"Well, skill never won the lottery," Jake said. "Have her keep at it."

Q's phone dinged with an alert. He swiped the screen and read. "Looks like a synthoid went MIA. On the west side. Jesus, from a daycare center."

"When?" EC asked, lighting up his *iSlate*.

"Not sure exactly. Reported missing yesterday, so it could have been anytime over the weekend."

"What shows up on the blotter?" Jake asked EC, watching him swipe the screen of his tablet.

"The usual mayhem. Nothing on the west side—wait a minute. Metropark Rangers found a body in the valley. But that's a shooting. Droids can't have guns."

"*Shouldn't* have guns."

"Right…Get this, the vic was naked except for a baseball cap."

Jake thought a moment then asked, "Shot six times in the chest?"

"Yup. Overkill, too. Not a likely Munchausen."

"But likely the Baron," Jake said.

"How's that?" Maddie asked.

"Search Aileen Wuornos W-U-O-R-N-O-S."

EC did, then read, "Aileen Carol Wuornos Pralle was an American serial killer who murdered seven men in Florida between 1989 and 1990 by shooting them at point-blank range."

"Victim number two."

"David Spears, age forty-three. Construction worker in Winter Garden. On June 1, 1990, his nude body was found along Florida State Road 19 in Citrus County, wearing only a baseball cap. He had been shot six times."

"Ah, you should probably know," Q said, "the missing unit from the daycare center…it was female."

Maddie whispered, "Welcome back, Jake."

***~~~***

# Into the Valley of Death

"Coffee?" Q asked after Maddie and EC left for the daycare center to investigate the missing synthoid. "Black, right?"

Jake nodded, then rested his forehead on his arms crossed on the conference table in front of him.

"You okay?"

"No. I ache like hell. Everywhere."

"Didn't they give you any meds for that?"

Jake gave Q a harsh scowl. "Junkies are junkies with junkie thoughts, whether you get it off the street or from Drug Mart."

Q nodded. He left to make two cups of coffee. He returned and slid a regular brew across the table to Jake, then sat down and sipped his own espresso. "At least these jamokes had a decent rig for their java."

"You know what hurts most?" Jake sat up again. "He's been right there within arm's reach the whole time."

"The guy's good."

"Yeah, but so am I. And nothing. No Spidey sense. Not a tingle. Man, he is one stone cold reptile."

"Unfortunately, he's so good, he knows how to go off-the-grid—really *off-the-grid*. Like I said, he might as well be pixels on moonbeams. And it seems like he's got the discipline to stay off, too."

Jake sipped his coffee. "Not bad, Marge."

"I'll bet you say that to all the geeks."

"Now, how are we going to get him?"

Q shrugged his shoulders. "I know there's something rattling around in all that silicon over there. But…"

"But?"

"But getting it out—intact…I don't want a nuclear meltdown."

"Well, we've got to get out in front of this parade. Fast. Playing catch-up is leaving too many dead bodies everywhere."

"But how?"

Jake pondered. "Dots. We're not seeing all the dots."

"Dots? What's *that* mean?"

"You didn't have a normal childhood, did you. Didn't your parents ever take you to a place with a kid's menu?"

"Like what? A *Cracker Barrel?* Yeah, right. In your dreams—and my nightmares."

Jake shook his head. He closed his eyes, leaned back, and rested his head on the back of the chair. "Maybe Kovacic's right."

"Come on, Jake. The SWAT guy? He's a meathead. What does he know?"

"Yeah…but if we can't get ahead of Jamal in cyberspace, we might have to do it the old-fashion way."

"How's that?"

Jake sat up and looked Q in the eye. "Out here. In meatspace."

"Yeah, well, just remember, I'm the guy with no kid's menu or crayon experience. You're on your own."

Jake sipped his coffee and stared into space.

Some called it the "Emerald Canyon." The Rocky River cut a deep gorge through the near west suburbs on its way to Lake Erie. After interviewing the owner, manager, and minder at the daycare center without getting much new information, Maddie and EC headed to the Metroparks Ranger headquarters, turning off Detroit Road and descending a hundred feet down to the Valley Parkway which followed the winding river upstream. Five miles in, the gorge opened up at a flood plain large enough for three golf courses. They pulled into the ranger station parking lot across from the Big Met clubhouse.

"Should we read this guy into our case or not?" EC asked before they got out of the car.

A pained expression crossed Maddie's face. "I don't like this."

"Like what?"

"Keeping these guys—and Derek—in the dark. I wouldn't like it. Neither would you. My dad always hated being treated like a mushroom." She sighed. "But I'm thinking not. Jake's right. At least not until we've got more than just a gut feeling to tie them together. I hate to do it, but maybe we should dump it all on Lt. Sands' desk."

"Fine by me. I didn't transfer into ACU for the politics." EC opened his car door and got out. "Besides, that's why he gets the office and the big bucks."

Maddie got out, and they headed towards the entrance. Two uniformed rangers and a husky middle-aged man in khakis and a sports jacket came out of the building and met them halfway.

"You the guys from downtown?" asked the man in street clothes.

"Detective Morgan?" Maddie asked.

"Yeah. Call me Wil."

"I'm Maddie. And this is EC." They showed Morgan their badges. "What's up?"

"Hiker just called in. Found a body out by Wallace Lake." Morgan took a long look at Maddie, then glanced at EC, and put his eyes back on Maddie again. He smiled. "Why don't you ride with me and we can talk. Your partner can follow us."

EC rolled his eyes and turned back towards their car.

Maddie fell in step beside Morgan. They got into an unmarked Ford *Explorer*. The two uniformed rangers pulled out of the parking lot with the roof lights on their patrol SUV flashing, heading south. Morgan pulled out behind them with EC in trail.

"So, what makes downtown so interested in our little murder in the park. Don't you guys have your hands full with big-city crime?" Morgan asked.

Maddie watched the trees flash by in a blur as the gorge narrowed and the bluff walls closed in again on the Parkway. "Wil, I'm going to level with you. Have you ever heard of Ailene Wuornos?"

"Nope."

"Neither had I until a few days ago. Wish I hadn't, but here I am. My lieutenant pulled me off my Robbery/Homicide cases and stuck me in with EC and his partner, because they have this idea that there's a copycat murderer loose in the city."

"And my case fits the pattern?"

"A couple of cases, actually. The naked guy in the ball cap and a woman's murder in Huntington Park."

Morgan looked over at Maddie. "That one's a few years old. One of our cold cases."

"EC's partner swears it's a knock-off of the Sam Sheppard case from the 1950s."

"That's a reach. Who even remembers that far back?"

"I don't know," Maddie sighed. "That's their working theory, anyway."

"Same guy?"

Maddie shrugged her shoulders.

"And your lieutenant is buying it?"

"That's what he wants me to figure out."

"Well…two bodies in one week is not exactly run-of-the-mill for us." Morgan looked at Maddie and smiled weakly.

"I don't want to get in your way. Just need to check out their theory. Satisfy the brass."

"You help us clear these cases, and I'll be grateful. Then I can go home at night and sleep again."

"No problem."

They drove in silence for a half-mile or so.

"So…how did you come to being on the job?" Morgan asked.

"Family business. My dad put in his twenty on patrol and retired a sergeant. My grandpa, too. I was supposed to go to law school, but…didn't," Maddie said. "I was always kind of headstrong that way. You?"

"After three tours in the sandbox, I thought a job as a park ranger would be good for my PTSD. You know, nice and mellow. Telling folks not to feed the bears and to make sure to put out their campfires."

"Marines? My dad was in the Corps."

"Army. Rangers."

"So, how's that plan working out for you?"

"Not so good…this week." Wil pulled into a parking lot by Wallace Lake in Berea and drove around to the three ranger SUVs with their lights flashing by a pavilion. He killed the engine. Staring through the windshield at the crime scene, he said sincerely, "I'll take any help I can get."

Maddie just nodded.

"Thanks."

EC parked behind them and came around to the passenger door. Maddie and Morgan got out and the three walked to the pavilion.

"What have we got?" Morgan asked the uniformed ranger who met them at the crime scene tape wrapped around the pavilion pillars.

"Hey, Wil." The ranger looked over Maddie and EC.

"They're Homicide from downtown," Morgan answered the unasked question. "Might be a connection to some of their cases."

"Got a male. Late thirties, early forties. No ID. Shot eight or nine times. Looks like a twenty-two. Maybe a three-eighty."

Wil shook his head and looked at Maddie. "Hell hath no fury?"

"It fits Wuornos," Maddie said.

"You might want to have the patrol guys start checking for abandoned cars throughout the park," EC said. "She totaled out at seven."

"Great," Morgan growled through his gritted teeth.

Each lost in their own thoughts, the three silently watched the Bunny Suit Boys process the crime scene for evidence. When the medical examiner's van took the body away, Maddie and EC went back to the city.

# The Invisible Mind

The bodies of four more men, all shot to death, would be found by the park rangers over the next week.

On the way home, Maddie stopped at the lakeside park playground used by the rogue robot's daycare center. She waited in her car until dusk swept away the last of the parents and children, then meandered around the slides and swings and jungle gyms, trying to see the world through synthoid eyes. Her thoughts inevitably drifted to orphan Amy.

A piece of paper flapping lazily on a posted warning sign caught Maddie's eye. A welcome distraction from disturbing thoughts, she walked over to see what it was. Her hand went immediately to the grip of her Glock, and she pirouetted to scan the park for danger. The area cleared, she turned back to study the paper, which held a collage of photos: Maddie coming and going at work…at home…at Jake's building…at the University Circle dormitory…at the Metroparks Ranger station…sitting at a patio bistro table at a Crocker Park bakery…standing outside the alley in the Flats where she had been attacked by the synthoid and saved by Jake. *Jamal…*

She went to the edge of the bluff and stared out to sea until night fell, fear and anger rooting deep within her subconscious.

# Stakeout

Exit Alley was deserted by the time Maddie finished her paperwork. EC and Samantha left together at six-thirty to get dinner. Q never came back from the Flats and his minions had cleared out at 5:01 PM like a migrating herd for happy hour at a virtual reality tech bar in the Warehouse District.

Maddie quickly tidied up her workspace on the conference table and left when the cleaning crew made their appearance. Instead of going home, she drove down the Shoreway to Lake Road, cut up by John's Diner, then cruised the alley behind the Glick Building before parking in one of the metered spots across Detroit Road from the dark storefront. She stared at the building like she had stared out across the lake at the park, haunted by the stalking of a serial killer. Jake's silhouette momentarily broke the steady glow from the second-floor windows, then moved away. Maddie rested her forehead on the steering wheel and closed her eyes. It didn't help.

She watched for another half-hour—maybe more—then drove around the building again. The tenant spots in the rear lot were empty, so she took one and went in the back way with the key she had from before. Frank scurried in between her legs. She followed him up the stairs to the second floor, took a deep breath, and went into the apartment.

"I wondered how long you were going to sit out there,"

Jake said, greeting Maddie at the door with a glass of wine. "Your stakeout skills need a little polishing."

"I—I didn't want, you know…" She took the glass and sipped quickly. "In case you had…"

"Company?" Jake stepped up and kissed Maddie's forehead. He put his arm around her shoulders and led her into the apartment. The living room furniture was littered with open books and stacks of papers leaving nowhere to sit, so they went to the kitchen. "You eat? I'm betting not."

She shook her head. "Did EC call you?"

"He did. You know, technically, he's still *my* partner."

Maddie sighed. She sipped, glancing nervously around the kitchen. "What have you got for food?"

"Just so happens, I went to the market and got a couple of slabs of cow meat from Mel." Jake pulled a platter with a pair of Delmonico steaks on it from the refrigerator and headed towards the back fire escape. "Come on, the coals are ready. Leave your Glock. Bring the Zinfandel."

Maddie went to Jake's bedroom and dug through his dresser for a pair of gym shorts and a T-shirt. She changed clothes, then, barefooted, joined him on the fire escape. "You don't mind I got comfy, do you?"

Jake looked Maddie up and down and smiled his approval. He shook his head, moved the baked potatoes to the side of the Weber, then threw the steaks on the grill.

Maddie sat down on the aluminum lawn chair and gazed out towards the lake, sipping her wine. "What are we going to do, Jake?"

"Um…about what, exactly?"

Maddie did not answer.

# The Invisible Mind

"Food fixes everything. So, first we eat."

After they finished the steaks, then emptied the bottle of wine, Maddie and Jake made love, just like old times.

Shortly after seven the next morning, Jake's phone rang, dragging him into consciousness. Maddie, naked beside him in his bed, moaned and rolled away when he answered. The caller was John from John's Diner. Waitress Amy had missed her second shift in two days, and he was calling to see if Jake knew where she was.

***~~~***

# Asylum Inmates

Without windows, Amy had long ago lost all sense of time, though through street-wise animal instinct could at least still tell when it was day and when it was night. So, she knew it was sometime in the middle of the night when the commotion of a struggle seeped through her prison walls. Muffled cries on the other side did not last long before they faded into whimpers, then silence.

She waited for what she reckoned was an hour before tapping lightly on the wall: Knock…knock-knock.

No response.

She tried again. Again, without reply.

She kept trying every hour until she sensed it was morning. Then stopped until night came again.

# Every Breath You Take

Jake sat alone at a booth up front in John's Diner. His third mug of coffee was half gone. He mindlessly watched the traffic on Detroit Avenue until EC arrived and sat down across the table from him.

"Coffee, hon?" Jackie came over and asked EC. After he turned over his mug, she poured. She topped off Jake's mug and said to him, "She's a good kid, you know. You better find her."

Jake just nodded, looking out the window.

"Thanks." EC smiled up at Jackie, then she left. He studied Jake over the brim of his mug. Three sips later, he said, "You didn't tell Maddie, did you."

"I did not. I figured it really wasn't the best way to start the morning." Jake sighed and looked at EC. "You know?"

EC shook his head. "No. Not really."

"Well, it's complicated."

"Yeah. I imagine. And you're a complicated guy."

"So everybody says."

"So…what now, *Kemo Sahbee?*"

"Simple. We get this guy."

"Gosh. Why didn't I think of that." EC sipped his coffee. "And how is that, *Mr. Complicated?*"

Jake pointed out the window to the traffic light at the intersection.

EC looked. It took a moment, then he understood. "The traffic cam?"

"And shoe leather." Jake smiled. "We can't just sit and wait for Q and his merry band of techies."

"Good ol' fashioned police work, then."

"I went to her apartment after Maddie left. It's at the west end, in the Mayfair."

"Was that an official visit or personal?"

Jake shrugged. "Looks like that's where she got grabbed up. And I'm betting it wasn't a 'droid. She's blonde, but not stupid. She wouldn't have let a stranger in. Not after all the shop talk I've shared with her."

"The Baron's not a stranger?"

"She knows I know Jamal. Seen me here with him. Jackie says he's been in a few times lately. Always sat in Amy's section."

"Oh. Great."

"It's been forty-eight hours. I told John to call the Lakewood PD and put in a report. Once it pops up in the system, we'll have some cover to start collecting video footage."

"Until then?"

"Let's take a walk and see what other eyes are on the street between here and the Mayfair."

Maddie got back to her apartment, made coffee, and lingered for a long while over a cup at her breakfast bar. *What a mess.*

Then her body reminded her how much she enjoyed being with Jake. How much she missed him physically, too. She could not suppress a smile. And all the messy complications of work and crime and relationships and death dissipated like fog in the hot rays of dawn piercing a clear morning sky. She savored a sunbeam warmth within herself.

It was later in the shower that a creepy dread bore into her as hard memories pushed back against her feelings. All the times Jamal had randomly appeared flipped through her mind like playing cards slowly dealt out at a mental blackjack table…and no longer seemed so random.

At the hospital when Sanchez died.

*But that was news, right? And he's supposedly a reporter…supposedly.*

Then at the "Hillside Strangler" crime scene off the Shoreway.

*News, again. And Jamal wasn't the only reporter there—but he was there before anyone else. And what about the video of her and Jake working the crime scene he showed them on the Darknet…*

In the station house, there making fresh coffee when she came into work at five in the morning before the shift change.

*Jamal and me…no one else around. He was there to talk about Jake. To warn me about Jake.*

On the patio at the bakery just down the street, after a morning run.

*Just down the street…*

In the alley in the Flats where the synthoid attacked her.

*I never saw him, but he was there…I know it…he was there…*

Maddie shut the shower off and hurriedly wrapped a towel around her body. She rushed into the master bedroom and grabbed her Glock off the nightstand, dripping water onto the rug. She stalked through her own apartment, methodically clearing all the rooms, until she ended up at the front window looking down on the street, wondering if the Baron was out there, watching.

She turned back inside and surveyed her apartment.

*Is he here…seeing her now?*

Maddie called Jake. He promised to come right away with EC, Q, and the gear needed to sweep her apartment for bugs, cameras, and IoT taps into her appliances.

The Baron would watch the last footage to come out of Maddie's apartment later, aroused by her nearly naked body dripping wet, armed with a semi-automatic pistol. But especially from the look of fear on her face.

***~~~***

# The War Room

Maddie, EC, and Jake waited downstairs while Q swept the Glick Building for cameras and microphones. No one spoke. Their phones, *iSlate*s and *iNodes* were in a shielded and hardened lock-box in the trunk of EC's unmarked car parked in the lot out back.

The two-story building was twenty-five feet wide and one hundred feet deep. Once home to his parent's flower shop, Jake had paid off his sister to take title of the property and began renovating. Upstairs was the three-bedroom apartment where he lived. Downstairs was hollowed out as one big room in the front sixty feet to be a huge mancave. Against the back wall was a complete kitchen, which featured a set of glass-fronted refrigerators from the old flower shop, now filled with beer and wine, and a twelve-foot long oak dining table. The rest of the room was filled with a plethora of distractions, including a pool table, baby grand piano, professional-grade surround sound audio equipment, kayaks stacked on a rack against the east wall, golf clubs, baseball bats, a well-stocked bar, and a huge sofa pit that faced a blank, white-washed portion of the wall for watching old movies. The rest of the exposed brick walls was covered with an eclectic collection of framed artwork, movie posters, and old concert handbills. The back third of the downstairs was a large workshop and garage area where Jake parked his classic black Ford *Mustang* convertible and his motorcycles.

Maddie and EC sat at the bar and watched Jake tape up a four-foot by three-foot detailed map of the city on the movie screen wall.

"Where in the world did you get that?" EC asked.

"Don't ask," Maddie sighed.

Jake turned and scowled at EC.

"Yeah, I know. I know. Radio silence." EC planted his chin in his palm and rolled his eyes.

Maddie silently shook her head.

Finished with the upstairs apartment and the back workshop, Q scanned the mancave under their watchful eye, then headed downstairs into the basement.

"You're clean," Q announced after another half an hour when he emerged from downstairs to declare the building clear of any unauthorized eavesdropping devices. "Now, we're going to have to keep it that way."

"How's that?" Jake asked.

"Really? You really want to know?"

"Humor me."

"We put a chastity belt on your meshnet authentication protocols and upgrade your encryptions with an Enigma XR module."

"Those are illegal, aren't they?" EC asked.

"The bane of national security and law enforcement agencies around the world." Q smiled broadly. "Thank you, Cartel IT department."

"You're right. I don't want to know," Jake said.

"All righty, then. Where's your router?"

Jake pointed towards the workshop.

Q disappeared into the back.

In the meantime, Jake joined Maddie and EC at the bar. "Once he's done, we can set up shop here. Just the four of us."

"Samantha, too," EC said. "She's been doing the heavy lifting on his profile."

Jake nodded. "But she keeps on working her end from Exit Alley. And Q will continue mining the server farm. We gotta keep chumming the digital river with activity to keep Jamal pre-occupied."

"Sands?" Maddie asked.

"Only if and when we have to. My guess is that he'd rather not know about it, so he doesn't have to lie to the Captain or Public Square."

Maddie and EC nodded.

"Now, the hard part."

"What's that?" Maddie asked.

Jake looked at her and grimaced. "We need cutouts."

"Huh?"

"It would be best if we can gather as much evidence and intel as possible without any of our fingerprints showing up on them. We need some fronts to put in the requests and pull that info for us."

"Who?"

"Maybe Wally. His Torso Murder case has gone cold. I'm thinking Derek from District Three. Mr. Ranger, Morgan."

"Why would they help us?" Maddie asked.

"Well, for one, how are the Speck and Wuornos cases going for those guys? From what I read in the media, about as well as Wally's."

"And?"

Jake looked at Maddie, then to EC. He rolled his eyes and nodded back towards Maddie.

"You dog," EC said to Jake.

"What?" Maddie asked.

Jake shrugged.

EC looked Maddie. "He thinks they may not be immune to your feminine charms and wiles."

Maddie scowled at Jake.

"It worked on me." Jake smiled.

"We're all buttoned up," Q announced as he came back from the workshop. He noted the staring contest at the bar. "What did I miss?"

Maddie got up and headed towards the rear exit. "Come on, *partner.*"

EC smiled at Jake, then followed Maddie out.

"Something I said?" Q asked.

*"Fuhgeddaboudit!"*

Jake went over to the map taped to the wall and began marking with a red Sharpie all the places he could remember being together with Jamal.

***~~~***

# A Little Help from My Friends

Maddie sat at a back booth in Cutty's Deli nursing an iced tea, angry as she usually was when she came around to the conclusion that Jake was right. *Again. Damn it. 'Cause we're in a race against time: Jamal has Amy.*

Her hair was in off-duty mode, unleashed from the usual tight pony tail or from being piled up and pinned on top of her head. It cascaded down and flowed over her shoulders like a wavy red waterfall, framing her face which now carried a bit more mascara and subtle shadow to accent her dark green eyes, accompanied by a deeper shade of red lipstick around her pouting expression. The extra makeup was added when she went back to her condo to change into leg-hugging jeans and a tight, low-cut top revealing the faint splash of freckles on her chest.

Cutty sidled up to the booth and leered at her over a long sip of Scotch from his CPD mug. "Miss…*Madeline?*"

"I don't want to." Maddie pushed her lower lip out even further.

*"Mmmmm…"* Cutty took another long sip, then offered his mug her way. "You need something a bit more, um, fortified?"

Maddie shook her head.

"Where's Jake?"

If her dark green eyes were lasers, two holes would have appeared in Cutty's forehead.

"Whoa. I just thought—"

"Sorry." Maddie's scowl melted back into child-like innocence, then bounced back into a sly smile as she spied Derek, the detective from District Three, coming up behind Cutty.

"Officer Cutler." Derek put his hand on Cutty's shoulder. It was quickly withdrawn when greeted with a glare as if it were pigeon droppings. "Maddie."

Cutty took a sip, eyeballing his goddaughter down the length of his mug, then stepped back to let Derek slide into the booth across from Maddie. "What can I get you, *detective?*"

"I'm off duty, thankfully. How about a Great Lakes Dortmunder?"

Cutty went back to the deli counter and sent a waitress over with Derek's beer.

"You look better every time I see you," He smiled and drank out of the bottle, his eyes never leaving Maddie's face.

She smiled back.

Derek slid his back against the wall and sat sideways in the booth with his leg up on the bench. He surveyed the smattering of deli patrons in for an early dinner before the rush. "So, your dad and Cutty, huh?"

Maddie nodded and sipped her ice tea. "Partners. On patrol."

"And you?"

She quickly fought back a reflexive wince. "I'm between—working with EC on temporary assignment."

"Sanchez…"

Maddie nodded.

"Tough break." Derek took a pull of Dortmunder, then set the bottle down. He twirled it on its bottom rim like a top. "And off the job?"

Maddie blushed and looked away. *Damn it.*

"Yeah, I'll let you take the Fifth on that one…*for now.*" Derek plugged his smile with the bottle.

"So…downtown, again?"

"Yeah, getting to be a too regular thing. Wish it wasn't, but, then again, here *we* are." He cocked an eyebrow her way. "At least my case isn't the lead story *every…single…day* in the news any more. Six bodies down in the Metroparks helped—at least for a little while."

Maddie recalled her similar meeting with Detective Ranger Morgan earlier in the afternoon. It was a much more straightforward conversation.

"But the hungry jackals will be back gnawing on my flea-bit carcass again. Count on it."

"Reporters. They all have their own little agendas," Maddie commented staring off into space shaking her head, thinking about Jamal. "Turn up anything yet?"

"A lot of busy work. Trolling the vics' online activity and accounts. Interviewing the dreck that gets dredged up. Their parents would likely be horrified at some of it, but, really, nothing that called for the archangel of death to visit. I don't know if we're going to find any connection there. Seems almost like a random bolt out of the blue."

"Physical evidence?"

"Nothing. The guy was a ghost." Derek sighed.

The right corner of Maddie's lips turned up slowly in a grim half-smile.

"What?"

"Nobody—I mean nobody wants to hear it. Maybe you don't."

"Hear what?" Derek sat up straight and turned to face Maddie squarely.

Maddie dug in her purse for her notepad and pen. She wrote "Richard Speck" on a page, tore it out, then folded it over, creasing it hard with her fingernails, then folded it tightly again. She placed the paper on the table and held it down with her fingers in front of her.

"You got something?"

Maddie shrugged her shoulders and stared into Derek's eyes.

"What do you want?"

She thought for a long minute, then smiled. "I'm kind of hungry."

"Dinner? I'll get the waitress."

"Not here. Someplace nice."

"Sure…the *Chop House?*"

"Mmmm, yeah. Steer meat." Maddie chuckled to herself, recalling Sanchez's disdain for men: *If we didn't need the calves, they'd all be steers in my book.*

"Okay. Deal." Derek reached for the paper.

Maddie held it down tight. "This probably isn't the help you want."

"I'll take any assistance at all that comes my way at this point."

"And…you'll help me, too, if I come to you."

Derek smiled at the thought of Maddie needing him. "Absolutely."

"Put this away and read it later. Then do the research." Maddie pushed the paper across the table and released it. "And maybe we can help each other."

Derek picked it up and held it in front of his face, turning it, and considering it from every angle. "Thanks."

"Just don't hold it against me."

"Never." Derek reached to take hold of Maddie's hand, but she pulled back.

"Now, put that away, so we can go get something to eat."

Derek stashed the folded paper in his wallet and they got up from the booth.

Cutty tracked his goddaughter as she left the deli with Derek. He put the detective's beer on Jake's tab.

***~~~***

# Suburbia

From behind dark-tinted safety glass, Jamal cast his eyes on the twenty-foot concrete wall along the interstate, allowing it to blur his passing and mask time ill spent as the self-driving car chauffeured him out to the suburbs. He much preferred walking. Sure, the fresh air was invigorating, but casually strolling through his near westside neighborhood or Gordon Square or Edgewater Park or even through the concrete and glass canyons downtown was, counter-intuitively, an active meditative state even better than his quiet time in the Faraday cage in his castle. Beta waves stilled themselves until his mind imitated a calm reflecting pool, opening the gateway to his subconscious to absorb sights, sounds, smells and even the contortions of the air all around from the mechanical turbulence of the wind or the microvariations of temperature due to both natural and man-made causes. He always came home filled with fresh ideas, the genesis of which he savored as a psychological mystery of religious proportions.

But exposing himself in public had become unacceptably risky as of late. He might briefly wander the backstreets and alleys around his lair in the middle of the night or disguise himself for an hour at eight AM or five PM to raft in the gushing ebbs and flows of distracted downtown workers swarming in and out of the Terminal Tower Rapid Transit station like ants. But the exhilaration at flirting with the danger of discovery polluted the calm pool of contemplation with adrenalin, leaving Jamal vaguely unsatisfied and somewhat irritable.

So now he rode out to the suburbs where he cruised the carefully planned subdivisions with their precise grids of residential streets named for all the trees clear-cut to create a middle-class utopia. He savored the illusion of order presented by the regularity of colonial, ranch, and split-level facades lined up along uncracked sidewalks cutting a proper border through unending meadows of closely cropped Kentucky bluegrass. He loved to imagine the chaos and mayhem bound and held captive deep in the closets, basements and attics of the prim and proper abodes. He smiled, because he knew murderers and serial killers were not unknown in this land, too.

*But he was a quiet, God-fearing, lawn-cutting, family-loving, neighborly-waving fellow…just like me.*

It tickled the dark heart of Jamal's soul.

But these regular joyrides also served a practical purpose, timed as they always were to slow-motion surf rush-hour traffic when the data load was highest on the highways due to the intense hive activity of Vehicle-to-Vehicle speed, direction and location streaming to maintain safe and orderly flow on the roadways. Due to the encryption hardening undertaken by automobile manufacturers to curb hackers from commandeering self-driving cars for "drone riding," it had taken nearly a decade for Jamal to crack the DOT transponder code protocols and develop the masking algorithms to use the shoaling commuters to hide his communications with the outside world via the Atlas Grid, necessary now that Jake and

Q had possession of the White Chapel facility and his own castle was connection-free.

He regularly pinged his embedded army of Munchausened synthoids to maintain an up-to-date census of serial killers-in-waiting. He checked in on Jake's investigation into *"The Baron"* through police department servers which, unsurprisingly, were as water-tight as the *Titanic* proved to be. He visited a closed DI-7 chat room in the seventh level of cyber-hell deep in the Darknet to read and post cryptic messages from and for the cabal of fans, supporters, and fellow travelers hunkered in the deep shadows of cyberspace.

Jamal was exceedingly pleased that Q had not yet taken the White Chapel server farm off-line so he could continue to pull down the re-gen code and park it in the NSA's online world where it could continue to propagate through the ecosystem of commercial data center service providers around the world.

Before he left suburbia and went off-line, Jamal confirmed the launch of data packets to activate his next murder by Munchausen.

***~~~***

# Fly Fishing

He almost missed it. A water bug's lightning quick skate across a calm pond. The faint stir of dorsal fin momentarily etched in the mirror of water above. The briefest spark of sunlight struck on silver scales to catch a kingfisher's eye.

At two AM, Q still sat on a stool deep in the dim alleyways of silicon, steel, and glass at the White Chapel building, bathed in the neon glow of a server monitor and his laptop screen. He was mining the database tiers again to gain entry to the Baron's impermeable virtual lair buried deep in a dark neighborhood of microchips populating printed circuit boards neatly lined up within their metal enclosures.

Bleary-eyed from hours of watching lines of computer code stream across his screen like whitewater rapids, Q thought his eyes were playing tricks on him.

*There it is again.*

He hit the spacebar on his laptop to freeze the video screen cap recording of the server monitor. He went back in near time frame-by-frame, then saw it. He was not going crazy. The flow of database coding was interrupted by the insertion of neural networking commands:

```
# Dense Layer
pool2_flat = tf.reshape(pool2, [-1, 7 *7 * 64])
```

```
dense = tf.layers.dense(inputs=pool2_flat,
units=1024, activation=tf.nn.relu)
dropout = tf.layers.dropout(inputs=dense,
rate=0,4, training=mode == learn.modeKeys, TRAIN)
```

Q video-framed forward, and the code insertion disappeared. It reappeared when he went back a frame, then disappeared when he went back a second frame. He went forward to expose the code again.

*"Damn."* Q slowly smiled. He pulled at the short reddish-brown hairs of his closely-cropped goatee, staring at his laptop screen. "You are sly…but so am I."

The code was a fragment of Tensorflow implementation of standard Convolutional Neural Networking, often used in the vision realm of artificial intelligence. It was a breadcrumb to track the Baron's trail into the Black Tier.

Q spent the hours until dawn fishing for more breadcrumbs and cataloging their memory registers to find the gate to the Black Tier and decrypt the key to unlocking it.

***~~~***

# The Epicenter

Jake sat back twenty feet in an old wooden wheeled office chair. He swiveled slightly to activate the squeak of ungreased bearings, staring at what had become a huge murder board in his mancave. The three-by-four-foot map speckled with red Sharpie dots held center stage on the white movie screening wall, a giant replica of a child's place mat with a connect-the-dots game. Laser printed pages of photographs surrounded the map like suburbs ringing the city. Each contained a gallery of victim portraits from past and present topped by a centered mugshot. Threads of blue sports yarn splayed out from the map connecting crime scene locations with each local victim's picture. At the far-left border of the whitewashed section of wall, copies of bygone hometown newspaper front page stories announcing the arrest of a serial killer terrorizing the community were plastered up next to a portrait of the lead detective. The far-right side displayed an anthology of the online local crime coverage of E.J. Quick. A step ladder stood nearby to reach the quickly vanishing white space left on the top half of the twelve-foot-high wall.

Jake heard the back door open, then close. He stopped swiveling to listen but did not look away from the murder wall. He recognized the ever so slight shuffle of Florsheim shoes on the oak plank floor. Footwear for the office, not the beat.

"Are we paying for all this?" Lt. Sands asked as he stepped up next to Jake and surveyed the wall filled with investigatory puzzle pieces.

"Just the yarn. I kleptoed Sharpies from the office," Jake answered.

Lt. Sands huffed a chuckle. He stepped up close to the wall to take a closer look at the photos. "So…you back up to full speed?"

"I'd say eighty…seventy to eighty percent."

"Good."

"You know, you and your fancy suit are standing in my way."

"Oh, gee, *sorry,*" Lt. Sands said, looking back at Jake over his shoulder. He turned to face the wall again and did not move away.

Jake sighed. He stood up and walked up next to Lt. Sands.

"What do you see?"

"Not what I need to—yet."

"And what's that?"

"The epicenter."

"Huh. Right. Interesting." Lt. Sands looked at Jake, then studied the portraits again. "I'm keeping my finger in the dike as best I can. But I've got this guy from District Three having a serious relationship with my voicemail."

"Derek."

"Yeah. Claims he talked to Maddie. He wants what you got—whatever it is. Bad."

"I don't think you want to do that yet. He's in the Director's office more than the shoe shine boy."

Lt. Sands nodded. "Who else?"

"A Metroparks Ranger," Jake said, tapping the mug shot of Aileen Wuornos. He pointed to the Kingsbury Run area on the map, where blue yarn led back to a picture of Eliot Ness above a series of gruesome crime scene photos of headless murder victims from the 1930s. "Wally in District Four. He's a good guy. He's been by, too. Knows the score and is all in. Haven't met Mr. Ranger or Derek, yet. I don't know. Might have to bring them in from the cold, huh."

"You know the score, Jake. We're out pretty far on this limb."

"Yeah. You keep saying."

"And if the bodies keep piling up…"

"You know the next one is out there, right? Even as we speak." Jake looked at Sands.

"Like I said, if the bodies keep piling up, we're going to have more help than we want. Whether we want it or not."

"More than we need. Nobody wants any suits from DC stomping around."

"Yeah. I know. But, seriously, where are we at on all this?" Lt. Sands waved his arm across the papers taped to the movie wall.

"You know about the kidnappings, right?"

"Kidnappings? Plural? Not just the kid?"

Jake nodded slowly.

"Great. You got something to drink around here?"

"There's some scotch behind the bar."

"Not the cheap stuff Cutty swills."

"Nah. Single malt Glenmorangie Signet."

"Thank you." Lt. Sands took off his suit jacket and hung it on the back of a bar stool. He loosened his tie as he went behind the bar. "You want one?"

"Nah." Jake sat back down in his squeaky chair and began swiveling—and squeaking—again.

Lt. Sands stopped mid-pour and threw a scowl Jake's way. "What, are you three years old? Cut it out."

"What?" Jake spun to look towards the bar.

Lt. Sands dragged a chair over next to Jake and sat. He sipped his scotch, pursing his lips as he savored the flavor. "How's Maddie doing?"

With a long drawn out squeal from the chair spring, Jake leaned way back in his chair. He put his hands behind his head and slowly shook his head.

"This isn't going to get even more complicated, is it?"

"This isn't complicated. It's evil—and that's pretty damn straight forward."

"It may be evil, but our day job is crime solving, not soul saving, and we got bodies stacking up as deep as snow in Buffalo."

"Those are just props—like the furniture on stage at the State Theater. They're in the play, but not part of the plot."

Lt. Sands groaned out loud. "Oh, man, don't ever be saying that to anyone outside this room, okay?"

A long silence hung between the two men.

"But it's true," Jake said softly.

"I know." Lt. Sands sipped his scotch. "But don't ever say that out loud, again. *Ever.* I won't be able to save you like last time and your career in law enforcement will definitely be over for good. As in roll credits. *Fin*…The End."

Jake just stared at the murder wall.

# Breaking Bread

Bill brought them down one-by-one. First the street urchin.

He watched Bill seat her to his right, nearly halfway down the absurdly long dining room table, first cuffing the D-ring on the back of the thick, pad-locked leather belt to the slats in the back of the chair, then her ankles to the front legs. Her handcuffed hands were separated by enough chain, threaded through a D-ring on the front of the belt, to allow her to eat, yet without permitting enough wind-up to throw any cutlery or glassware—at least not very far or to any great effect. Jamal smiled ever so slightly at the heat of the glare Amy threw his way.

This was Amy's first opportunity to put eyes on Jamal since her abduction before the raid on the White Chapel building in the Flats. Once the video was made to taunt the police, he locked her away alone in the castle safe room. She studied her captor's face as he slouched back in his chair at the head of the table, his smile hidden behind the steeple of index fingers above clasped hands, pressed against his lips. A bland, yet eerily calm expression masked his thoughts, though his deep black eyes met, welcomed, and seemed even to embrace the hatred in Amy's glare. Amy did not comprehend what their staring contest was about, but she could feel herself losing.

Jamal felt no arousal but saw in Amy's finely sculpted features and rich brunette hair that she would one day mature into a strikingly exotic beauty…*if allowed.*

Bill brought the waitress, shuffling submissively, to her place setting on the left. Her blonde hair hung down about her bowed head, shrouding her face. After being shackled to her chair, waitress Amy stared down into her empty plate.

Amy unlocked from Jamal's eyes to look across the table at her fellow prisoner, whose half-closed eyes gazed into an abyss beyond her empty plate like a dazed junkie. She began to fear what she, too, might become.

The waitress was also pretty in a suburbanly girl-next-door kind of way, Jamal thought, *but not quite worthy of a pedestal like Maddie or the grown-up version of the young orphan.* He sat up straight in his chair and in a soft, smooth baritone voice greeted his guests, *"Ladies…*I trust you have brought your appetites."

He nodded to Bill, who went around the table filling their wine glasses with a blood-red Cabernet. He placed the bottle in front of Jamal, then retreated to the kitchen.

Jamal smiled warmly at the surprise on the young orphan's face. He nodded.

Amy hesitated halfway in her reach for the wine glass. She looked to head of the table, as if for permission.

Jamal lifted his own glass to encourage her on.

She brought the glass close to her lips. Sniffed, then gingerly sipped.

Jamal swirled his wine as he watched closely the youngster's exploration into adulthood, then tested the wine himself.

Waitress Amy aroused from her stupor with a jerk. She grabbed her glass and gulped, stopping only when she inhaled instead of swallowed. She coughed hard into her arm, nearly spilling her wine.

Jamal looked, then turned back to the youngster to his right and rolled his eyes. She responded with a hurried second sip.

Bill came out of the kitchen with a tray of lobster bisque. He served them and left.

"I trust you have been well taken care of by Bill and Stephanie," Jamal said.

"I don't know why I am here," waitress Amy said in a hoarse whisper.

"We are here to break bread and enjoy a special meal. Stephanie is quite the culinary artiste."

"No. *Why am I here?*" she whined.

"Life is suffering, my dear…" Jamal tested his bisque and smiled. "But there is no reason for it to be completely unbearable. Please. Try your soup. I hope neither of you are vegetarian. We're having medallions of beef tenderloin with peppercorn sauce, wild rice, and a lemon broccoli that is simply delicious. I do not know what her secret is, but it is amazing. And that is just the vegetable."

"What are you going to do with us?" orphan Amy asked softly.

"That, I am afraid, is a chapter that has not yet been written." He looked at the young girl. "Please. Eat. Do not let your bisque cool."

She set down her wine and tried the soup.

Jamal again savored the child's reaction to her first taste. He turned to waitress Amy. "You, too.

After they finished, Bill magically appeared to clear their bowls.

"You are aware, of course, of your…um, *utility,* shall we

say." The Baron sipped his wine, then asked orphan Amy, "Do you know our friend, Jake?"

She shrugged.

"Well, perhaps, you are not aware of his deep feelings for the red-headed detective who took you off the streets." Jamal turned to waitress Amy. "I am sorry. But you do know how he feels. Deep down. Right?"

Waitress Amy replied with only a heavy sigh. She stared at the empty space where her bisque had been.

"But what does that have to do with me?" orphan Amy asked.

"Well…"

"You can't just do this to people—to us," waitress Amy sobbed.

The Baron smiled. "Oh, but I can. In fact, I have."

Waitress Amy shrunk back into mute submission.

"But why?" asked orphan Amy.

Jamal smiled as he scratched at his new, closely-cropped beard, contemplating the question. "Why do you live on the streets when there is no reason to? After all, Miss Madeline saw to it you were placed safely, comfortably in a nice home in the suburbs."

"I dunno."

"Hmmm…I think perhaps you do, but you will not admit it."

Orphan Amy shrugged.

"It is hard—harder living that way. But…" The Baron leaned in to look directly into Amy's eyes like a stern father. "Tell me the truth. It is hard, yes? But it is more…*real.*"

Amy stared back, then gave a quick nod.

# The Invisible Mind

"Precisely. For quite some while now, our lives—everyone's lives have become increasingly *unreal*—broken down. Fragmented. Self-pixelated, if you will." Jamal sat back and smiled at his own allusion. "All fancy themselves as digital deities—avatars—it is Hindu, you know. One really must admire the utter *hubris* of even the most common of mankind. *They are worthless.* To themselves. To everyone. Can they look you in the eye? Can they even truly understand another anymore? Or do they even care to. I think not."

Waitress Amy looked up quizzically.

Jamal stood and picked up the bottle of wine. He went to her side and towered over her. "Do you understand what I am saying?"

The blonde slouched back in her chair, crossing her arms over her breasts. She shook her head and stared at the wine pouring into her glass.

"Mmmm. I did not think so." Jamal walked around the table to orphan Amy. As he refreshed her glass, he said softly, "But I believe you do. Deep down. Though you may not see it, yet. For, you know, we are quite alike. Much more than you think."

She reached for her wine as soon as he lifted the bottle away to mask herself with a sip.

Jamal emptied the bottle into his own glass and sat back down at the head of the table. He stared into his wine and spoke in a rising voice, with a harsher tone, "Their white picket fences will not—*cannot* hold back hell from the purgatory of their own making behind all the false facades of their petty, soulless profiles."

His anger reverberated back fear on their faces as both girls stared towards the head of the table.

The Baron sipped his wine, then in a calm, quiet voice said, "And so purgatory shall be purged."

"What do you mean?" asked orphan Amy meekly.

"If they refuse to seek, then you bring it to them." Jamal sighed. "As you well know, reality has great cleansing properties. So, you bring it to those who refuse to partake."

Bill entered the pause in conversation to serve their entrees.

"So, let us break bread, then," Jamal said in his soft, smooth baritone voice after Bill left the room. "Please, eat. Enjoy."

And the three ate dinner in silence.

***~~~***

# M.I.A.

Maddie and EC waited in the sumptuous reception area of the Stein, Baylor & Stein law firm outside the elevators on the thirty-fourth floor of the Tower at Erieview. EC perused artwork valued in the millions in the huge gallery of a lobby, strolling and pausing in front of original oils and watercolors on the walls and pedestaled sculptures as if he were visiting the Cleveland Museum of Art.

Maddie found and sat in the lone stuffed leather chair positioned to allow a sliver of a view of Lake Erie through the glass walls of the lobby, down a long hall and through the open door of a much-coveted partner's office facing north. Storm clouds gathered over the water. Whitecaps pushed relentlessly toward shore. Maddie watched blankly, lost in that moment of time until the feel of a colony of ants on her calves presaged the tsunami of a hot flash that hit her like a breakwall. She closed her eyes and waited for the inevitable ebb. After, her mind backfilled with thoughts of the young girl she had tried and failed to save from the dangers of a life on the streets in the Flats. Fear for Amy in the hands of the Baron stirred the vortex of these internal storms.

Someone at Stein, Baylor & Stein called to report one of their Personal Services Assistants, used for file and document retrieval, had gone missing. Such a call was unusual—like citizens too embarrassed or guilt-ridden to report their handgun being stolen—even though it was required by federal law. Civilian owners and operators typically turned to private tech firms to trace and track their errant synthoids. Most times, the disappearance resulted from a programming glitch in the unit's location services algorithms. Annoying, but harmless. Less frequently, larceny was involved, which made it a matter for Robbery/Homicide. But truth be told, android bounty hunters gave those disappearances a much higher priority than detectives who were already swamped investigating crimes committed by and against humans, which Maddie knew first hand. Besides, the private sector more often produced results with the prompt return of the missing PSA before it was smuggled out of the country or run through a chop shop for its parts and precious metals. When a malware hit for ill intent was suspected—as Lt. Sands feared in this instance—the case was referred to ACU, which he did forthwith without the usual bureaucratic routing of intake paperwork, instead calling Maddie directly to send them there in person.

A tall blonde woman in a tailored business suit came to the door of the lobby to escort them in. "Come this way, please."

Her beauty made even Maddie stare.

Without introduction or chit-chat the woman led them to a small, darkly paneled and windowless conference room. "Donald will be with you shortly."

EC stared at the closed door and whistled.

Maddie cleared her throat. "And Samantha?"

EC shook his head as they sat on the side of the table facing the door. "I've still got a pulse, you know."

*Men.* Maddie just smiled.

Precisely three minutes later, Donald marched into the room. "Please, officers, don't get up."

Maddie, who made no move to stand up, deduced from the military-style cut of his sandy-colored hair, perfect posture, muscular build, and impeccably bland dark suit the firm had probably recruited Wilkinson from the Secret Service.

EC stood to shake his hand.

"Donald Wilkinson, Vice President of Security Services for the firm."

"Maddie." She shook his hand with a demur smile. "In the Corps?"

"No, ma'am. Navy. SEALs."

"And after?"

"The Department of Homeland Security."

*I knew it.*

Donald sat down across from EC and Maddie. He folded his hands on top of a manila folder. "So, to what does Stein, Baylor and Stein owe the pleasure of this visit?"

"The firm recently reported a missing Personal Services Assistant unit," EC explained.

Donald looked at EC. He looked at Maddie and smiled broadly. "So, to what does Stein, Baylor and Stein owe the pleasure of this visit?"

"Why would you ask?" Maddie reached out and tapped the top of the manila file folder. "I assume you are aware that a report was made."

"Of course. It is a federal regulation for any civilian owner and operator of synthetic humanoids to do so. And Stein, Baylor and Stein is a legal firm which, of course, holds itself to the highest standards of integrity. I am just curious as to why this particular report—unlike the two prior made by our firm and the dozens made by or handled on behalf of the firm's clients—has finally brought the police to our door. In the past, these matters were dealt with…directly, privately."

Maddie looked at EC, then sat up straight in her chair, arching her back and folding her hands together on the table in front of her. The smile left her face. "Mr. Wilkinson—"

"Please. Call me Donald."

*"Mr. Wilkinson*…We are not from Robbery/Homicide. We are not here concerning the possible theft of your PSA. We are from the Artificial Crimes Unit, which investigates felonies perpetrated through the illicit use of synthetic humanoids. And the report provided by Stein, Baylor and Stein was, let's say, perfunctory with very little investigatory information of value."

"Surely, you don't think the firm—"

"We do not." Maddie sighed heavily. "Can we be assured of the firm's cooperation in keeping our conversation completely confidential?"

EC whispered at his partner, *"Maddie…"*

Wilkinson looked from Maddie to EC, then back to Maddie.

"I can arrange for you to speak with our commanding officer, if you like. But…you should know, time is of the essence in our investigation. And lives are at stake."

"I am intrigued." Wilkinson sat back and smiled.

"Do we have your cooperation? And Stein, Baylor and Stein's?"

"Yes. Of course. How can we help you?"

"You are aware, of course, of the murders of nine nurses in University Circle and the six bodies found recently in the Metroparks."

The smile evaporated from Wilkinson's face. "I am."

"You are probably not aware that a child and young woman have been kidnapped."

The executive's face hardened into that of a former Secret Service agent whose character and personality had been razed and rebuilt by the Naval Special Warfare Command on the sandy beaches at Coronado, California.

"Have you employed the services of a recovery agent?"

"That is something we handle with in-house staff."

"Excellent. When can we meet with your team?"

"Wait here, and I'll arrange for it directly." Wilkinson got up and left the conference room.

"Maddie, do you think this is wise?" EC asked.

"I don't know. But we'd obviously be wasting our time otherwise." Maddie put her elbows on the table and rested her forehead against her fingers.

The door opened. EC's blossoming elation at the reappearance of the blonde who led them there quickly wilted as she was followed in by a waiter pushing a serving cart of coffee, soft drinks, and pastries. *"What the hell…"*

The blonde was brought up short by the unexpected greeting.

Maddie looked up and stared the food service synthoid directly in its cold, artificial eyes as it stood at attention beside the cart, awaiting their beverage selection.

"Mr. Wilkinson said he would be a few more minutes yet before he returned. Would either of you care for refreshments?" She noticed Maddie staring at the PSA. "Right, then. I'll just leave the cart. Please, help yourself. Roland, come with me."

"Unbelievable," EC said after the pair left.

Maddie just shook her head.

EC got up and inspected the assortment of cookies, bite-sized brownies, and mini cannoli. "Do you want anything?"

"No, thank you."

The conference room door opened. Wilkinson held it open for a tall, thin, white-haired authority figure. He was followed in by a veritable black-haired clone of Wilkinson, then Wilkinson himself. The door was quickly pulled closed.

"Officers. Welcome. I am Lance Baylor, senior partner." He greeted Maddie and EC each with a nod in their direction, then went directly to the food cart and poured himself a cup of coffee. "Donald, here, has filled me in on your earlier discussion. The firm appreciates your forthrightness. I will see to it that you have the unfettered assistance of our firm to help resolve this unfortunate situation as quickly as possible."

"Thank you," Maddie said.

"However." Baylor sat down directly opposite Maddie, flanked by Wilkinson and his clone. "We need assurances of reciprocity with regards to confidentiality. Then, we can have the most productive conversation for the benefit of all."

"For a robot file clerk?" EC asked.

The question hung in the air as Baylor focused his full attention on Maddie, awaiting an answer to his proposition.

She slowly nodded. "Certainly."

"Very good." Baylor sipped his coffee.

"The missing PSA was no mere file clerk," Wilkinson explained. "As do other firms of our size, with our involvement with major corporate entities, we handle many confidential matters with regards to trade secrets, mergers and acquisitions, joint venture negotiations, and the like, so we must be sensitive to any and all attempts to breech attorney-client privilege. We are careful not only in implementing secure communications protocols, but often times we find it necessary to camouflage the movements and meetings of our client principals and our partners, so as not to leave breadcrumbs for others to map their activities and thereby draw conclusions about the intents of our clients. Sometimes, it involves masking the N numbers of corporate jets in flight plans, making safe house arrangements for face-to-face meetings, and…" Wilkinson looked at Baylor, who nodded, then continued. "And, in this case, using PSAs as secure couriers of legal documents."

"You can well imagine, then, our concern for confidentiality in this incident," Baylor said.

"Exactly what kind of documents?" Maddie asked Baylor. "And where were they being delivered?"

"It was the final, executed agreement for a, um, major business acquisition for one of our wealthier clients," Wilkinson said.

"Who is that?" EC asked.

"The who is not important," Baylor said curtly. "It is the *what* which has us most concerned. You see, the documents were being delivered with the private key for a cryptocurrency payment to complete the transaction."

"How much?" Maddie asked.

Baylor sighed heavily. "Four hundred and fifty million dollars."

"*Holy cow.*" EC whistled.

"Quite."

"And you just sent this droid off into the world on its merry way with four hundred and fifty million dollars?" Maddie asked.

"First of all, fail-safe procedures were implemented in the event of a hostile act against the unit's will—I mean, of course, in violation of its preprogrammed mission profile—which purges the secured memory locations holding the data and keys and overwrites them seven times," Wilkinson explained defensively. "So, there is nothing physical to steal except the synthoid. And an act of theft would trigger the fail-safe protocol."

"And second?" asked EC.

"Of course, the delivery was monitored electronically from our operations center here, as well as being physically shadowed by human operatives."

*Wait for it,* Maddie told herself. She smiled. "But…"

"Somehow, the unit mistakenly got into the wrong *Uber* for the route segment to the airport Sheraton drop location and disappeared."

Wilkinson's dark-haired clone bowed his head, leaving no doubt who would take the fall for the breach in security.

"The wrong *Uber?*" Maddie looked at EC incredulously.

"We have a corporate contract with them for Level One secure livery services." Baylor said. "We've never had any issues in the past. Ever."

"I don't think that was the wrong *Uber,*" EC said.

"It was the wrong one according to our plan," Wilkinson argued.

"Yeah, well, Custer had a plan, too," Maddie mocked. "And so did Crazy Horse."

EC chuckled at her quoting one of Jake's more well-worn retorts.

"I think someone else had a plan, too. And that someone hacked and hijacked your unit. So, if this 'Plan B' was not sensed as a hostile act?" Maddie asked, looking at Baylor, then Wilkinson.

"Then the fail-safe protocols may not have triggered," Wilkinson revealed.

Baylor sighed. "So, the contract and crypto key would remain intact."

"And the Baron now has four hundred and fifty million dollars." Maddie closed her eyes. She felt the lava-like heat and pressure of another hot flash building toward eruption within her chest.

***~~~***

# The Tears of a Clown

Jake met Lt. Sands at the crime scene. "This is no coincidence."

"No. No, it is not." Lt. Sands sighed. "One block further west, and it's out of our jurisdiction."

They stared at the sheet covering the victim's body which had been dumped beside the railroad tracks behind the GFS store on West 117th Street.

Jake looked down the tracks west, towards his apartment, then to the east.

"Don't worry. Norfolk and Southern is holding their freight traffic until we're done here," Sands said.

"Where's Maddie?"

"I want you on this one. You and me."

*"Okay…"*

Lt. Sands motioned over the Coroner's tech to pull back the sheet, revealing the naked body of a woman in her twenties.

The first thing that caught Jake's eye was the face garishly painted like a clown. He stepped over and leaned in to more closely examine her circus mask, then looked up at Lt. Sands.

Lt. Sands pointed to the victim's chest.

Jake looked down and saw that the left breast had been removed. "Oh."

"Yeah."

Jake took out his phone and snapped a picture of the victim's face. He did a photo search. "Huh."

"What is it?"

Jake stepped back over to show Lt. Sands the results. "Pretty close match.

Lt. Sands looked at the picture on the phone, then the victim. He looked at the phone and pointed to the face on the screen. "Who's that?"

"Pogo the Clown."

"Again, who's that?"

"Also known as John Wayne Gacy. More than thirty killings. In Chicago."

*"Damn."*

They looked back at the dead woman.

"But this is not his MO. And definitely not his preference in victim," Jake said.

"Men?"

Jake nodded.

"So, what does this mean?"

"I don't know." Jake shook his head. "I don't know."

A second body was found later that afternoon east along the railroad tracks on Whiskey Island. A third body was discovered near dusk on the other side of downtown where the railway passed Gordon Park. Both victims had been mutilated in the same way with their faces made up to look like Pogo the Clown.

***~~~***

# Search and Recovery

Q couldn't quite believe it when he first saw the unencrypted incoming video stream at the server farm. Hands methodically folding and neatly stacking a coat, blouse, skirt, stockings, and shoes on a beach. Then, a semi-automatic pistol carefully placed on top. He saw the orange and white "crib"—the municipal water system intake station four miles out from shore—as the view panned the horizon from the deep darkness west to the soft pink glow of sunrise behind the downtown skyscrapers to the east. Waves lapped at the beach. A slow march towards Canada began. Sand gave way to nothing but water, rising step-by-step, until the splash from cresting waves blurred the lenses on artificial eyes. Then, a few murky moments before the feed went dark.

His gut knotted hard. Even an inanimate death is unsettling.

Q called Maddie.

She met EC at Edgewater Park. They called the Coast Guard, then bagged and tagged the pistol and each item of clothing. By the time all the evidence was collected, inventoried, boxed, and locked in the trunk of EC's *Crown Vic,* a medium response boat ringed in orange searched in close to the shoreline. Forty-five minutes later, an orange helicopter arrived from the Coast Guard Station in Detroit.

EC parked himself on a bench to watch the chopper fly an ever-expanding search grid over the lake.

Maddie went back to the beach to amble along its length and back, just beyond the reach of expiring waves.

Rush hour traffic on the Shoreway had dissipated when the helicopter began hovering over the east end of Whiskey Island. Maddie watched as the motorboat gunned its twin outboard engines and banked around in a tight U-turn to speed off to the east. Twenty minutes later, the helicopter headed north. EC got a phone call and waved Maddie back. She followed his *Crown Vic* to the Coast Guard station downtown between Burke Lakefront Airport and the Rock and Roll Hall of Fame to meet the search boat.

The female synthoid brought ashore strapped to the stretcher was still eerily life-like. It's Dermaloy skin had not wrinkled after all the hours in the water. The open eyes were unhazed, their blue-gray color still clear. There was no smell of death, just lake. A demur smile taunted the detectives.

EC called Puff and Bob from the Technical Forensic Lab to come retrieve the unit.

Maddie called Morgan at the Metroparks Ranger station. "It's over…at least for you."

"You sure?" he asked.

"We found a Bersa three-eighty with lavender grips with the body—I mean, the synthoid. Well, among the effects left behind. Anyway, I'm willing to give odds that the ballistics will match the park victims. I'll let you know for sure when I get the report."

"Thanks. What do you need from me?"

"A little more time to get our guy."

"You getting close?"

Maddie sighed. "Closer."

"Sure. I'll hold 'em off as long as I can. But you know how the powers-that-be are sometimes."

"Thanks. I appreciate it."


When they got back to Exit Alley, Derek from District Three was there in the parking lot, leaning against the front quarter panel of his car. As Maddie and EC approached, he called out, "You promised me, you know."

"Go on," Maddie said to EC.

"You sure?"

"I'll be there in a minute."

EC shrugged. He watched back over his shoulder as he walked to the entrance, then let himself into Exit Alley with the evidence from the beach.

"Hi, Derek." Maddie smiled. "What brings you downtown?"

"I thought we had, you know, *an understanding.*" Derek smiled back. "You haven't been returning my calls."

"Perhaps you *mis*-understood our understanding."

"A nice dinner. Fine wine. I even sprung for dessert. Then?" Derek wagged his finger at Maddie. "Crickets. What's a guy supposed to think?"

"Are we talking shop, here? Or…"

"Hey, Derek," Lt. Sands called out. He stood at the door to Exit Alley flanked by Jake and a linebacker-sized man with a crew cut. "Thanks for coming."

*Saved by the bell.* Maddie smiled and waved at the trio.

"To be continued?" Derek asked Maddie.

"Come on. Let's get started." Lt. Sands waved them over.

"Hi, Wally," Maddie said to the Detective from District Four who was investigating a Torso Murders copycat. "Find any new headless horsemen, lately?"

"No. Not lately." Wally chuckled. "Good to see you, too, though."

Lt. Sands held open the door.

"Hi, Jake," Maddie said as she breezed by, followed by Derek and Wally.

Jake sighed, then went into Exit Alley.

Lt. Sands squeezed, then roughly patted Jake's shoulder from behind as they walked to the small conference room.

Q, Samantha, and EC were already seated around the table. Maddie quickly grabbed the seat next to EC closest to the head of the table where Lt. Sands would conduct the meeting. Jake sat next to Q at the far end with Derek and Wally.

Lt. Sands held up his phone and powered it down, then pushed it towards the center of the table. "Ante up, everybody."

When everyone's phones were off on the table, Lt. Sands sat down.

"You didn't bring in Morgan from the Park Rangers?" EC asked.

"We're going to keep it in the family for now." Lt. Sands pointed down the table at Derek and Wally. "Jake's painted the broad strokes for you guys and the ACU tie-in to your cases. Right? Synthoid copycats of Speck and the Torso Murder case."

They nodded.

"Well, we've had three more victims show up within a twelve-hour period—one west side, one downtown, and one on the east side. Based on the coroner's estimated TODs, highly unlikely that there is only one AnSub. Probably three. Not even AI is smart enough to figure out how to be three places at once."

"But one of them could have done the nurses, though, huh?" Derek asked.

"Possibly, but..." Lt. Sands looked at Q.

"Possible, but not likely," Q said. "At least not without reprogramming. He's replacing the personality and occupational specialty libraries with the specifics to recreate past serial killers. First, he'd have to flush and refresh repeatedly, which is more likely to leave metadata markers in the Atlas Grid. Second, the only two synthoids reported missing so far are the au pair and the law firm's unit. I think he may be returning them after the crimes to keep them *on* the grid—hidden in plain sight."

"And the female droid washed up on Whiskey Island this morning," Maddie said. "The date-time stamp on the video stream puts her at Edgewater within twenty-four hours of the latest murders, so it's a possibility for the downtown victim, but unlikely. The au pair's spree in the park was with a gun. All men and no mutilations. Totally different M.O."

"What have you got on these latest ones, Jake?" Lt. Sands asked.

"The clown faces are definitely Gacy—John Wayne Gacy. A Cook County serial killer in the Seventies convicted of thirty-three killings." Jake passed a set of pictures around the table.

"What's the clown deal?" Wally asked, looking over the painted faces of the victims.

"Get this, the guy used to dress up like Bozo and do kids' birthday parties and fundraising events. He'd even march in holiday parades," Jake answered. "But Gacy's victims were all teenage boys."

"But these latest vics are all women," Lt. Sands said.

"So, what gives?" asked Derek.

"He's taunting us."

"Who?"

"The Baron. The amputation of the left breast is the signature of another series of Chicago killings by a gang of four Satan worshipers called the Ripper Crew. Suspected in the murders of eighteen women."

"And the Gacy connection?" Maddie asked.

"Gacy was in the construction business and the leader of the Ripper Crew, a guy named Gecht, did some painting or spackling or something for him as a subcontractor."

"So, we're three-deep into a series of eighteen," EC said.

"Yup. And like with Speck, the Ripper Crew only got caught 'cause one of their victims inadvertently survived and later IDed them." Jake shook his head. "The Baron's not going to let that happen again."

"And there are two, if not three, AnSubs on the loose out there," Lt. Sands said. "A major escalation—and this is on top of two abductions, which we still haven't figured out how they fit in with the Munchausen murders, right?"

Jake and Q both shook their heads.

"So, you two…" Lt. Sands pointed at Derek and Wally. "Are now part of our rag-tag task force. We gotta stop this guy. Fast."

"Does corporate know?" Jake asked.

"I've briefed the Chief one-on-one. Whether he's told the Director yet is his call, but I don't think he'll carry the weight on this for long, so we need to figure out a plan, cause I'm sure Reagan is going to have some hard questions on all this once he finds out. Q, what have you got?"

"The Baron has to still be communicating with the Munchausened units somehow to activate them. He used to wormhole through NSA servers, but there's nothing popping there, so he has to have found another channel."

"And the server farm in the flats?"

Q glanced quickly at Jake beside him. "Nothing, yet. There's something in there in a heavily firewalled and encrypted tier. I just haven't breeched it yet."

Lt. Sands looked at Jake, then back to Q. "Do it. Just get it done. Jake, what have you got off the wall?"

"Off-the-wall?" Jake grinned.

Lt. Sands replied with a no-nonsense look.

"Still connecting the dots. My gut says he's a westsider. Activities are slanted that way."

"Figure it out. Pronto. Okay, EC, you coordinate the tech side. Vet through what Samantha's come up with in her profiling and put a damn gun to Q's head—if you have to—to crack those servers. Wally, you're with Maddie on the au pair and Stein-Baylor angle." Lt. Sands looked down the table at Jake and smiled. "Jake…Derek here is going to help out with the Ripper Crew murders."

"Yes, sir." Jake saluted.

"Don't call me sir."

"Yes, sir."

"Remember, there's a woman and a young girl who need to be found, ASAP. Find the Baron and we'll find them—*before it's too late.*"

The room went silent.

"Well, what are you waiting for?"

The meeting quickly broke up and the teams went their separate ways.

***~~~***

# Destroyer of Worlds

Amy's stomach growled with hunger. When the key hit the door, the youngster sat up eagerly at the edge of the bed, ready to receive her dinner wondering why it was so late. But when the door opened and Jamal came into the room dragging a bentwood chair behind him, she reflexively pushed herself back against the headboard and pulled her knees up to her chest.

The Baron set the chair at the end of the bed and sat. He smiled at Amy.

Bill came in behind him with a bottle of wine and two glasses on a serving tray. He poured a splash into one of the glasses and handed it to Jamal, who swirled, sniffed, sipped, then nodded his approval. Bill poured a glass and handed it to Amy. He filled Jamal's glass then left, closing the door behind him.

Jamal saluted by cocking his glass in Amy's direction.

Amy took a quick gulp of wine.

"Now, child…" Jamal's voice was soft and smooth. "You are young and still…petite. Sip and savor."

Amy nodded. She took a dainty sip.

Jamal drank. His steady gaze unnerved the child, and she drank again. "Have you heard of a man, a man named Oppenheimer? A scientist, actually."

Amy shook her head.

"Not surprising. No, I suppose not."

"What do you want with me?"

Jamal bounced with a slight laugh. "No. Not what I want of you. What is it *you* want?"

"To go home."

"Home? And where, exactly, is home?"

Amy cast her eyes into her wine and sipped.

"Precisely. You know, we are not so much unalike, you and I."

"Yeah? How's that?"

"In the end, it is of little matter. Except, for you to know that. And remember it."

"Okay."

They sat, only their sips scratching softly at the silence between them.

"So, this Oppenheimer. He fancied himself a destroyer of worlds. And though he did, indeed, terrorize an entire generation of human beings on this planet with his…discovery, he ultimately failed in his god-like pretensions. After all, here we are—still. No?"

"He sounds like a bad guy."

"Mmmm, no. Not really. You know how sometimes the smartest geniuses in the world are the dumbest people in the room? They have the world before their eyes—even in their grasp—and yet remain unconscious to its true meaning."

Amy shrugged. "Are you a bad guy?"

"I am sure there are many who most sincerely believe I am. But those who might also spend their lives denying pain and misbelieving evil to be an imperfection in the world their perfect God created. It is not."

"Are *you* a destroyer of worlds?"

"No. I am not a god. More like…a lowly agent of change."

"What change?"

"You have chosen, right? You return to the streets again and again to live a hard life—much harder than need be. Why?" Jamal sipped and waited, but Amy did not answer. "The story is as old as stories themselves. In suffering, there is redemption. The only real truth each and every one of us all see in complete clarity is pain. It is a primal truth. It is truth without words. The truth before words."

"Are you going to hurt me?"

The Baron smiled. "No. I'm here to save you…if I am allowed."

"I—but…"

He savored the chaos of Amy's thoughts etched in confusion on her face. Jamal stood and picked up his chair. "I'll send Stephanie in with your dinner."

***~~~***

# The Floater

"You'll like these guys. They're a hoot," Maddie said to Wally as they got to the door of the Technical Forensics Lab.

"Colorful characters are they?"

"You could say so."

Wally held open the door for Maddie. "After you, darling."

Maddie smiled and entered. "Hi, boys."

"Well, well, well. Looky here, Puff. We got company." Bob abandoned his partner leaning over the female synthoid at the workbench. He extended out his hand to shake. "I'm Bob. That there is Puff."

Puff waved a Phillips-head screwdriver without looking up.

"Yeah. I'm Wally," he said, looking around warily at the robot heads, hands, and feet dangling from the ceiling against the walls and spilling out of plastic bins on the shelves. "So, Bob, how do you guys decorate for Halloween?"

Bob looked around. He chuckled. "Welcome to ghoul town, friend, where every day is Samhain."

"If it's not Scottish, *it's crrrap,*" Wally said with a heavy brogue. "I had a feeling about you guys."

"Criminy crackers, already." Puff looked up from the android torso. "We're on the clock here, people. Teatime ain't until four."

"Don't let him fool you," Maddie whispered to Wally. "He really missed me."

"I heard that, young lady. The only missing I'll be doing is all of you people at happy hour—*Not.*"

"Now, Puff. Where's your manners," scolded Bob. "He's just cranky that you called us out of the lab first thing this morning, before he had a chance to finish his coffee."

"Sorry, Puff. But what's a poor girl to do when she's in need of help?"

"Yeah, well, dang it all," Puff grumbled. He pointed down at the synthoid pulled out of the lake. "So, what's the deal with Mary Poppins, here?"

"Mary Poppins?" Wally asked. "Really?"

"Yup. Really," answered Bob. He looked up earnestly at Wally and adjusted the wire-rimmed glasses on his nose. "Funny thing most folks don't know is that when this whole deal was just getting off the ground, the android guys in the Valley secretly went to their Hollywood buddies down south and licensed up as many characters as they could—especially from beloved old G-rated classics. See, they figured that if the units resembled familiar faces from the big screen, that John and Jane Q. Public would subconsciously feel more comfortable having robots hanging around them all the time. We ran the feature set ID and this one was modeled on an actress named Andrews from the mid-nineteen hundreds."

"As in Julie?" Wally asked.

"The very one."

"Sure, sure. Makes perfect sense for daycare work."

"Oh, no. Don't tell me you're an old movie buff, too?" Maddie asked Wally. *Just like Jake.*

"You should see my collection. I've got a copy of the original *Mary Poppins.*"

Maddie shook her head in silence.

"Hey, *Professor.* You done with your damn lecture yet?"

"Cool your jets, there, Puff. Most folks like hearing a little inside info."

"I get my fill of shop. I don't need no talkin' about it—and yer yappin' ain't making my day go any faster."

Bob shook his head and rolled his eyes for Maddie and Wally. "See what I put up with."

"So, what have you found so far?" Maddie asked.

"This one ain't no mermaid," said Puff. "Droids and water definitely don't play nice together."

"Damaged bad?" asked Wally.

"Just lucky it wasn't salt water."

"Of course, first off, we pulled the Three Laws chip," Bob said. "Tested bad. Ran the manufacturer's serial number, and it's actually supposed to be installed in a unit registered to the Naperville Household Hazardous Waste Facility near Chicago."

"Don't tell me," Wally said. "That synthoid is present and accounted for."

"Yup, yup, yup. Pulled the cert records from the database for this A-VIN. Mandated inspection was done last September by NEOdroid Services in Brookpark. It all seemed to be in order, but then we ran the license number of the tech who signed off on it."

"And he's deader than this here floater," said Puff. "Hit by a bus and kilt, four years ago."

"Yup. So, we called and NEOdroid said they farmed the work out to—"

"White Chapel," Maddie said. "In the Flats."

"Yup."

"Should have known." Maddie looked at Wally. "The Baron's lair—or used to be—until SWAT took it down. That's where Jake was attacked."

"That's about all we know so far," Bob said. "It'll take us some time to dry things out and pull the data for Q's gang."

"And we'll know a whole lot more a whole lot quicker if you get out of our hair already," Puff stood upright and squinted at Maddie.

"I missed you, too, Puff," Maddie whispered.

Puff's scowl melted ever so slightly at the corners of his lips and eyes.

***~~~***

# Partners

"Totally iced-out place," Derek said as he prowled around the perimeter surveying Jake's mancave. "So, do people ever wander in off the streets thinking they can buy stuff—what with the storefront and display windows and all?"

"Used to. Especially just after Mom and Pop's shop closed down," Jake answered. He tossed his keys on the bar. He went around and grabbed a couple of bottled waters out of the refrigerator. "Most of the locals know better. A few stop by for a beer instead. You know, in the summertime when the door's open. Most give the shield a wide berth."

"Lots of nefarious activity out on the streets?"

"No more than usual, particularly later in the evening around the bars. But, hey, live and let live. Even dog catchers get to clock out at the end of the day."

Derek circled back around and met Jake in front of the murder wall. He took the water Jake offered, cracked off the cap and drank. "So…you and red, huh."

Jake smiled. "Yeah. We were partners."

"Were?"

Jake just smiled.

"Her dad retired out of the uniform, right? Him and Cutty. Thick as thieves—or so I hear."

"You checking up on her?"

"Just doing my homework. You know, due diligence and all." Derek took a long pull off his water. "Wouldn't you?"

"Harry was my training officer."

"Oh, so you go way back with the family."

"I got…*history.*"

"Hmmm. Interesting choice of words." Derek winked at Jake. He stepped over to the wall and started reading the postings. "So, I take it the jumbo-sized murder board is here to keep the NSA and SVR from poaching and solving our cases right out from under our noses. A little paranoid, don't you think?"

"Q swept the joint and hardened my net connection. So, we're good." Jake parked himself in his old office chair and started rocking slightly to excite the spring's squeaky sweet spot.

Derek looked over his shoulder at Jake.

"It's not the spooks on the federal payroll who are worrisome. Or aren't nine dead nurses enough to give you pause?"

Derek turned back to look again at the wall. "And you and Sands and Q and all the merry little digital elves are convinced it was a 'bot?"

"It seems a safe bet. Fits the serial killer copycat angle we got going on."

"Spree killer. That's what Speck was. Technically, anyway."

Jake stopped rocking and the chair went silent. "That all you got so far in your investigation?"

Derek's shoulders slumped. *"Touché."*

"And, technically, the F.B.I. says you need more than one location for a spree killer. So, what you got there for yourself is what we in the trade call a *mass* murderer case."

Derek's head bowed.

Jake started rocking—and squeaking—again. He tried to scan the murder wall around Derek, who began shuffling back and forth to read the different pages taped around the map of the city.

Derek hummed an unfamiliar meandering melody as he read.

Jake gave up and swiveled away from the wall.

"Lots of windy city connections up here," Derek said.

"Huh?"

"Speck…Gacy…that Ripper Gang. How many serial killers were there in Chicago, anyway? Sounds like a pretty dangerous place."

"Chicago?"

"And sweet Jesus. Eliot Ness, too? I don't see Al Capone up here. What's the deal with Ness?"

Jake swiveled back to face the murder wall. "He was Safety Director here during the Torso Murders—Wally's copycat case."

"Gruesome stuff. Lucky him."

"The Ripper Gang…Jack the *Ripper*—of course."

"Of course, what?" Derek turned and looked at Jake.

"Mudgett. *Damn it*. Come on."

"Where are we going?"

"Cutty's. You drive."

On the way downtown, Jake called EC to meet them at Cutty's Deli, then stared out the window lost in thought.

EC was already there in the usual back booth. "Hey, Jake. What's up."

"Might have a break." Jake slid in across from EC. "Thanks to Derek."

"Me?" Derek stood at the end of the booth.

"Yeah?" EC slid in to let Derek sit next to him.

"It was right there. Right in front of my face. D*amn it.*"

"You're welcome, I guess," Derek said. "But what'd I do?"

"Is Samantha having any luck on her profile?" Jake asked EC.

"Slim pickings. The guy's like vaporware—not really there, you know? Or anywhere."

"Tell her to start scrubbing records in Chicagoland—you know, the city, Cook and Dupage Counties. Maybe even Gary, Indiana. But particularly the south side. Around Jackson Park."

"Okay…What's she looking for?"

"Holmes. Jamal Holmes. Especially juvie records, CPS and Family Services. Get Q to help crack them if they're sealed."

"That's his last name? Holmes?"

"And maybe some kind of Biblical 'E' name. Elijah, Ezra, Ezekiel, Emmanuel."

"E.J. I get it. But what's Sam going to find?"

"I don't know. But that's where she's going to find it. I'm sure of it."

"Why's that?" Derek asked.

"You caught it. Not me. Too many Chicago connections."

"Ness and all the serial killers?"

"And the infamous player-to-be-named-later," Jake said.

"Who's that?"

"Maddie's case. The hookers in the Flats. That was Jack the Ripper."

"He's not from Chicago," Derek smirked. "I still don't get it."

"Jack was the first serial killer ever. Our first—the American Ripper—was Herman Mudgett—"

"What the hell kind of name is Mudgett—especially for a serial killer?" Derek asked

Jake looked and sighed. "Also known as H.H. Holmes."

"Also, from Chicago," said EC.

"You got it."

"And you think there's a connection with the Baron?"

"I think he thinks there is. And that's what is important."

"I'll get Sam on it right away. Let me out."

Derek got up to let EC leave. He sat back down across from Jake.

"Thanks, Derek." Jake smiled.

"You're welcome…I guess."

"Now, buy your partner lunch," Jake said and waved Cutty over to the booth.

***~~~***

# Parkour

Q laced his shoes tight. He slipped on a gray hoody with the Tampa Bay *Buccaneers* flag—his adopted hacker logo—then a Navy "Top Gun" baseball cap turned backwards and a pair of Ray-Ban brown-gradient Wayfarer sunglasses. He bounded down the stairwell from the second floor of the warehouse, bursting out the emergency exit at the end of the building in the Flats. Waving to the patrolmen in their black cruiser parked at the front entrance, Q loped off south to the river, taking the path of most resistance, vaulting retaining walls, climbing up and around and over iron bridge trestles and jumping completely up and down over stairways, sometimes using center handrails with his feet in a perfectly timed stride to extend his leap.

The late afternoon sun drew a stretched-out cartoon silhouette that flailed comically on the ground parallel to the trail Q blazed along the river around Oxbow Bend, back to the north. He crossed the Cuyahoga River and continued along the shoreline under the Main Avenue Bridge, down the boardwalk and through the malls and plazas of the upscale Flats East Bank, dodging pedestrians now as well as architects' esthetically pleasing exterior renderings made real out of brick and concrete. At the boardwalk's end, he easily scaled a security fence, crossed the railroad tracks at the lift bridge over the river, then sprinted out to the Lake Erie shoreline. He sat to catch his breath facing the gap in the breakwall where an ore boat hovered in the water pointed up stream like a Paul Bunyon-sized steelhead.

Q gazed at the northern horizon for a long while, his mind temporarily cleansed by the improvised urban obstacle course. His discovery, though, slowly swelled again like a mental boil, pressuring his thoughts painfully. To the west, the sun neared the water. He rose and began the long walk back to the warehouse.

In the sepia induced in the Flats by the sunset and his Wayfarer lenses, Q saw a figure leaning over the driver's side of the police cruiser, head bobbing in conversation with the patrolman behind the wheel. *Of course. But how? How did he know?*

"Get it out of your system?" Jake stood up and asked as Q approached.

"Eh, you know how it is." Q pulled off his Ray-Bans and gave Jake the once over. "You're looking better."

"Yeah. Funny how sometimes the best medicine is no medicine."

"You want to come upstairs?"

"I thought you'd never ask." Jake turned towards the cruiser, reached in and squeezed the driver's shoulder, a reflex habit to check that a fellow officer was wearing his bullet-proof vest. "Thanks. And you guys stay safe out here."

Q led Jake up to the second floor and NFCed them into the server room with his police ID. "I reprogrammed the locks after the door was fixed."

"Now you're thinking. Man, kind of…tropical in here." Jake took off his jacket.

"Yeah, the cooling and venting is totally inadequate for the thermal load."

"It's an old building. Like mine." Jake stepped over to the window. "These don't open, do they?"

Q shook his head.

"Okay. So, what are we *not* talking about, already?"

Q took a deep breath. "The Baron, he's left-handed, isn't he."

Jake looked out the window and thought for a long moment, remembering times spent with Jamal. He turned back to Q. "Yeah, he is…*So?*"

"That's what I thought. Artistic."

"Well, he's a writer, though I never found his pieces particularly arty."

"No, not really that. I mean left brain-right brain, stuff. Right-handed people are left brain dominant. That's the verbal, rational, orderly side. Lefties lean to the right hemisphere."

"Can we cut to the chase?"

"Since I can't read it directly, I've been mapping and modeling the Black Tier. You know, like unexplored territory. It's like satellite imagery, not like actually pounding the pavement. But…no, maybe more like an MRI."

"Enough with the similes. What's the map look like?"

"It's definitely a brain simulation."

"How good?"

"Damn good. Hellaciously good."

Jake stared at Q. "Who's brain? Jamal's?"

"Maybe mostly. To start. But, now it's also a little bit of Speck's and of Wuornos' and the Ripper gang guys. It's growing experientially. We're not dealing with just an outbound push to the synthoids. There's a sensory return loop, too."

"The videos."

Q nodded. "And…*it dreams.*"

"Dreams? Seriously?"

"I may not be able to see what it's doing, but I can watch how it's doing it. So, I've been tracking the server metrics for a while—power consumption; I/O; CPU, memory and graphic engine loadings; bandwidth consumption; RPS, ARTs and PRTs—"

"English, please."

"Requests per Second. Average Request Times. Peak Request Times—*But,* the point is, there is a circadian clock-thing going on. At night—which is actually during the daytime for us—"

"Right. Graveyard shift."

"You did not just say that."

Jake shrugged it off.

"Anyway, during the sleep cycle the left hemisphere is quiet, except for random internal pixel, video and audio waveform transfers from the right side. Like how we dream. Our unconscious sends over crazy video clips of ourselves in weird situations with people we know that leave us scratching our heads when we wake up in the morning—but they somehow make sense. You know, the whole Freud thing."

Jake reflexively looked to the left side of the server room.

Q chuffed. "There's no real spatial left or right…I mean, *I don't think there is.*"

"And during the day—I mean night. The machine's day, damn it, then what happens?"

"It starts…you know, thinking. Rationally. Increased thread counts, heightened CPU utilization, increased network packet transfers."

"Network transfers? Like to the Grid? I thought you said this thing was cut off from the outside world."

"Yeah…not so much, really. I lied to Sands."

"Well, that's gonna be between you and him. I'm not management. Does it help the case?"

Q nodded.

"Show me."

***~~~***

# The Bar Maiden's Death

The synthoid waited in the dark, narrow space between the dumpster and the building behind the bar. Odor sources had been cataloged and dismissed as non-relevant to the downloaded mission profile. The distance from where it stood to the bartender's parked car had been measured to the millimeter by laser and the transit time had been calculated in milliseconds. CMOS optical sensors auto-calibrated themselves to the ambient light in the alleyway. The noise gate on audio input was reduced to -48 dB to maximize listening sensitivity.

The unit's day job was walking through and inspecting intercepts for the Northeast Ohio Sewer District, so it was already dressed in Tyvek coveralls to protect from blood splatter. The map of city sewer lines resident in its memory would guarantee an untraceable egress from the crime scene through the predesignated manhole nearby. It waited with infinite patience and absolutely no trace of anticipatory anxiety. At two AM, the synthoid's readiness state escalated to Condition Orange. One thousand, three hundred sixty-eight seconds later, the rear entrance to the bar opened.

Target confirmation by facial recognition. Blonde. Five-foot, five inches tall. One hundred, twenty-six pounds. And alone. The bar maiden never made it to her car.

The synthoid's hydraulic grip around the throat

immediately silenced her by crushing the windpipe. Lifted off the ground by the neck, arms and legs flailed futilely, then eventually went limp with the loss of consciousness. A series of weak tremors through her body preceded her death.

The synthoid threw the body over its shoulder and quickly, stealthily moved north to the Norfolk and Southern railroad tracks, then west. At the preprogrammed navigation waypoint, the course turned back south and terminated in the alleyway behind the Glick Building. There, the corpse was stripped naked and the left breast was removed with a boning knife to be discarded in the sewer where rats would make quick work of it.

Jake woke before dawn with crazed blue and red beacons from police vehicles dancing on the walls and ceiling of his apartment. Through the back window, he looked down and saw a pair of patrolmen reeling out yellow tape to establish a perimeter around what was obviously—against the black asphalt of the parking lot—a female Caucasian victim. He dressed and went downstairs.

"Morning, Jake," said the Lakewood Police sergeant supervising the scene when he walked up. "Sorry to wake you."

Jake stared at the blonde hair, then the wound where the left breast should have been. He inhaled slowly, deeply. He closed his eyes, looked up, and blew audibly between his pursed lips.

"You didn't happen to hear…or see anything did you?"

Jake looked back down at the victim. He shook his head.

"Hell of a thing. Poor girl."

"I'll leave you to it." Jake turned and went back inside.

*** ~ ~ ~ ***

# Chicago

"Hey, Cutty, what time is it?" Jake asked after he stepped into the deli and surveyed the dining room.

"Almost ten." Cutty replied from behind the counter.

"How long has she been here?"

Cutty followed Jake's eye-line to his usual back booth. "Oh, almost a half-hour. Why? You late for a date?"

Jake smiled. "No. Actually, I'm right on time for a change."

"I'll be damned. Better get myself square with the Pope for the end of days."

"Yeah. You do that." Jake went over to the coffee service station and poured himself a mug. He watched Samantha's lips move as she read off the screen of her *iSlate*. She was rehearsing, but he didn't want a canned presentation. *She probably has a PowerPoint, for Christ's sake.* He smiled behind a sip of coffee and walked over. "Sorry I'm late."

Startled, Samantha looked up. She nervously checked the time on her screen. "Oh, no. You're right on time."

"Well…whaddaya know." Jake sat down in the booth. "Thanks for coming."

"Um…oh, sure." Samantha tucked her wavy brunette hair behind her ears. "You look tired."

"Just an early morning commotion in the neighborhood." Jake looked her over. "It's nice."

"Huh?"

"Your hair. You've had it done. Used to be straighter. Longer, too. No?"

Samantha nodded, looked down, and rearranged her silverware. "Thanks for noticing."

"EC like it?"

"Yeah. He does."

"Quite becoming." Jake took a sip of coffee. "You finished the profile, right? What does EC think about *that*?"

"He said it's good. Quantico quality he claims, but…I don't know. He's sweet."

"Yeah. He's like that. Could you please send it to me when you get a chance?"

"But—but don't you want to go over it?"

"Let's see, male…twenty-five to forty…highly intelligent…loner from a dysfunctional family…in and out of trouble as a *yute* with a minor juvenile record—sealed of course…probably dropped out of college, but has managed to establish and maintain a steady, if somewhat erratic, employment history—I think I'm really close on this one, no?"

Samantha, crestfallen, nodded her head. "Then, why—"

"Have you eaten? Cutty makes the most amazing blintzes."

"Oh, no, really. I'm fine. I should probably get back—"

"Nonsense." Jake waved over their waitress. "Hi, Emma. Breakfast still being served?"

"You know it is, Ace," Emma snapped back.

"Great. Come on, try them."

"No. I shouldn't. Maybe just a fruit cup."

"Nonsense. There's berries on them. That counts. Trust me. Get them."

Samantha caved and nodded. "Blintzes, please"

Emma wrote, then pointed her pen at Jake.

"And I'll have my usual: dry rye, a scoop of cottage cheese and a grapefruit—gotta watch my girlish figure, you know."

"Honey, don't trust this guy any further than you can throw him," Emma said to Samantha. "An order of blintzes and one kitchen sink omelet with extra crispy hash browns, whole wheat toast—extra butter--and a large OJ coming up. Cottage cheese and grapefruit, my ass."

After Emma left, Jake smiled at Samantha. "Trust me, you won't be sorry about the blintzes."

Samantha sighed heavily. "So, how did you know about Chicago?"

"It was Derek who connected those dots."

"And the fact that his real name is Holmes?"

"Now, *that* was me. I don't think Derek has a clue about who H.H. Holmes was. Not exactly the studious type, that guy."

"You know, I'm embarrassed to say it…but in a way I kind of feel a little sorry for him. Is that bad of me?"

*Eureka,* Jake thought. He looked Samantha in the eye and said softly, "For him, the kid? No. He was just a kid then. Not a monster yet. How could you not?"

"I mean, his mom getting killed in a drive-by gang shooting when he was only seven."

"And mom was on her own, right? Dad was M.I.A."

Samantha nodded. "It looks like he tried—tried really hard, but nothing ever seemed to work out for him. It's not clear why."

"The system is a hard place to be. Bad enough as an adult, but especially when you're a child. You know how vicious kids can be. They're nothing but half-tamed beasts."

"That's probably why he kept running away and going back to the old neighborhood. Lived on the streets, at least in the summertime. I don't know what he thought he'd find there, because there was no other family."

"You think he went back to avenge his mother?" Jake asked.

"Hadn't thought of that. Maybe. It might fit, 'cause he somehow got caught up in the rivalry between a couple of gangs. But she was no angel—that's for sure. Her sheet is a long one: possession, theft, prostitution. In and out of clinics, but I guess the methadone never worked for her. She always went back."

"What was her name?"

"Evelyn."

"Huh…" Jake couldn't suppress a crooked half-smile.

"What?"

"Excuse me, folks." Emma served their breakfast, then filled Jake's coffee cup. "Can I get you folks anything else?"

"Thanks, but no thanks." Jake smiled. "Not right now."

Samantha poked at her blintzes until Emma walked away. "I'm scared for those girls he's got. Really scared. Especially the young one. What is he going to do with them? To them?"

"You know more about Jamal than any of the rest of us. What are you afraid is going to happen? That's he's going to rape and sexually abuse them?"

"If you go by the F.B.I guidelines—and there is the whole thing with the…the mutilations."

"Forget the F.B.I. And the Baron doesn't own those mutilations. That's copycat, signature business."

"I don't know. Maybe not. I keep thinking about the little girl. Could he…"

"No. I don't think so."

"Why?"

"Don't get me wrong. They are very much in danger. He could kill them and may well do it…if he hasn't already. But this is not about—this is not a sexual thing."

"How do you know?" Samantha stared directly at him.

"I can't say—I mean I don't know how I know. I just know. Trust me." Jake held her gaze and whispered, "Trust me."

Samantha nodded and shrugged her shoulders. "What choice do I have?"

"Come on, let's eat. Try the blintzes."

They ate in silence.

"You were right," Samantha said. "These are good."

"E.J. Holmes, right? Did you find out what the 'E' stands for?"

"Yes. Enoch."

Jake froze in mid-bite. He dropped his fork to his plate.

"What? It was some prophet from the Old Testament."

Jake picked up his coffee and drank. He looked away, around the dining room.

"What?"

Jake looked back. He smiled and shook his head. *"Son-of-a-bitch."*

"What is it?"

"This isn't about sex. Not at all. He's on a mission."

"Mission? What kind of mission?"

"Damn it, I don't know." Jake sighed. "Could you go back and double check whether Evelyn was really his mother or if she might have been his grandmother?"

"Why?"

"Please? Just humor me."

***~~~**

# Amy

Jamal entered the room, dragging his bentwood chair noisily across the floor.

*Not again,* she thought from beneath the quilt. She heard him firmly plant the chair at the end of the bed. She felt his presence over her, then the chair creaked a bit as he sat. She lay still, pretending to be asleep, but knowing it would not work.

"I know you are not sleeping."

With a huff, waitress Amy rolled on her back and pulled the quilt off her face. She stared at the ceiling. The smell of coffee teased from the mug he had silently set on the nightstand.

"It is a beautiful morning," Jamal crooned in his low baritone.

"Yeah? How would I know?"

"I just told you."

"Yeah, well, thanks for that." Amy sat up and reached for her mug. The chain between the bed frame and the cuff on her ankle clinked. "You've made my day."

"You amuse me."

"Super."

"Was Jake so amused?"

Amy snorted and took a drink of coffee.

"I wonder…"

Amy waited. "What?"

"Do you think he has been faithful to you while…while you have been with me?"

She scowled.

"Hmmm…just a passing thought."

"What do you want?"

"What do any of us want? To be treated justly. Rewarded fairly for our sacrifices."

"Yeah. So you've said—*repeatedly.*"

"Yes, of course. Too bad in this world it is rarely so."

Amy's brow furrowed in thought.

Jamal smiled. He drank from his mug.

Amy put her coffee back on the nightstand. She threw back the quilt and swung her legs off the side of the bed.

Jamal watched closely.

Amy slowly unbuttoned the top of her pajamas. She slipped it off her shoulders, letting it fall free from her arms. She turned towards him, naked from the waist up.

The Baron's smile wilted. He was at once aroused and repulsed at the temptation before him.

"I could…" Amy listened to the deepening of his breaths. "…if I were fairly rewarded…"

Jamal sat back and smiled. "So…you would betray him."

She said nothing but met and held his stare.


In the next room, orphan Amy let Stephanie brush her hair. The first few times, she resisted, but once she gave in, came to crave the small act of kindness. She liked being cared for. She liked how Stephanie told her she was a pretty young child. Amy liked listening to her softly hum melodies as she tenderly pulled the brush through her hair. Today, though, the woman was silent.

# The Invisible Mind

"Miss Stephanie…what is it?"

"Nothing, child. Nothing."

"He isn't going to hurt me, is he? I don't want to die."

"We all pass, but not until our time."

"But I don't want to."

"Don't you fret, child. Don't you fret."

"But—"

"I have a nice, new dress for you. I'm sure you'll like it. You will look so very pretty."

Amy nodded but felt herself fill with dread.

"Don't you fret, child. Don't you fret."

***~~~***

# The Invisible Mind

Q lay on his back on the cot he set up in the server room, staring at the ceiling. He waited for the bells to start clanging on the antique windup alarm clock he brought from home. Nine minutes or so later—the old mechanical clock was a little fuzzy in its timekeeping—the alarm on his phone would go off at precisely the time it was set for according to the U.S. Naval Observatory Master Clock. They were both unnecessary now, as Q's natural sleep cycles were finally in sync with the Black Tier.

He sat up and grabbed a hand full of Fruit Loops out of the cereal box by the cot. The sugar fix perked him up. He grabbed the box and went over to roust his laptop out of sleep mode.

"Oh…no…" Q said out loud, even though he was the only one in the building.

He sat down and watched in dread as the graphs on the server monitoring app updated, showing a massive tsunami of outbound network traffic, which redlined three hours prior—w*hile I was sleeping.*

Just as Q was about to start investigating, his phone dinged with a text message:

> My Dear Companion — Thank you so much for keeping me company, but the time has come for me to be on my way. Attached is the encryption key to what

you seek, but, alas, there is no longer much to find there. Not even breadcrumbs. Until we meet again, warmest regards, The Baron.

Q used the key to unlock the Black Tier and confirmed its data drives had been wiped clean. He shut down his monitoring app.

His phone dinged again. It was an alert from his sniffer algorithm. The Baron had sent the Munchausen instruction set for the next Ripper Gang killing in the clear.

Q called Lt. Sands to warn him, then forwarded the text to Samantha.

He shut down his laptop and waited ten minutes, then called Jake. "Did you talk to Sands?"

"Yeah, he just called," Jake answered. "We figure somewhere along the Nickle Plate Road. Maddie and Wally are taking the east side. Derek and I will cover the west tracks. Sands is calling Lakewood, Rocky River, Bay, and Westlake to have them step up patrols out their way. Do you have an A-VIN on the synthoid? Can you track it?"

"I sent the info to Samantha to work the trace and trap. But Jake…"

Jake stayed silent on the other end.

"I think it's a diversion."

"What do you mean?"

Q explained the data dump, the Baron's text, and the empty Black Tier.

"Did you tell Sands?" Jake asked.

"No."

Silence on the line. "Good. Call me if there's more."

Q replied with a nod of his head.

# The Invisible Mind

"Q? You there?"

"Yeah, Jake."

"Call me. You hear?"

"Of course."

Q tossed his phone on the table beside his laptop. He grabbed a folding lawn chair and went up to the roof. He looked north and saw where the "Crooked River" passed beneath the Detroit Superior and Main Avenue bridges on its way out to the lake.

Q opened the lawn chair and sat, trying to imagine the invisible fury which had been unleashed on the world while he slept.

***~~~***

# The White City

Jamal and orphan Amy sat on a bench by the Fountain of Eternal Life in Veteran's Memorial Plaza downtown where caretaker Bill had dropped them off in the big black *Denali* SUV. She wore her new dress and a delicate layer of makeup Stephanie had applied which made her beauty glow. Amy's wrist was handcuffed to Jamal's.

Before they left, he warned her not to cry out for help and held a handgun up within an inch of her face to emphasize the point, an unnecessary gesture. He told her no one would care and no one would notice and most likely no one would help—at least not in time to save her—but she already knew that cold, hard reality well. When she lived on the streets, Amy always felt invisible. No eye contact or smiles, winks or nods. *Invisible*.

After being locked up indoors for so long, Amy savored the breeze on her face and the warmth of sun on the back of her neck. She was back in her natural element. Jamal held her hand in a warm, firm grip which, ironically, made her feel safe and relaxed. Surviving on her own meant always being on guard against human predators. She might be his captive, but the Baron would protect his possession.

*At least I mean something to someone.*

They sat in silence. Soon, the outflow of downtown workers from the buildings began, human rivulets joining into streams to puddle at bus stops and in parking lots for the evening commute home to the suburbs.

The Baron smiled. He looked all around and shook his head.

"What is it?" asked Amy.

"The ripple effect." He pointed at the fountain. "You would do well to consider how such small splashes can reach so far."

"What do you mean?"

"This place here where we sit, the Mall, reminds me of long ago. Of home."

"Where's that?"

"Chicago. It is a ripple from 1893. Look at them. Most people do not even have a clue."

"A clue about what?"

"Note these buildings." Jamal pointed to the library and the United States Courthouse to their right, then the old Board of Education Building and Public Hall on the other side of the Mall. "Classical architecture. Big white buildings lined up in neat rows. City Hall and the County Courthouse at the other end. The landscaping. Open space. Beautiful views, all the way to the lake. And a certain symmetry to it all. A ripple from long ago"

"Is this, like, history stuff?"

Jamal shook his head. "It reminds me of home. That's all. They copied the World's Fair to beautify their own cities. But we're all copycats. It's what human beings do." Jamal checked his watch. "Speaking of which…come, child."

He stood. He smiled down on Amy and gently pulled her up to her feet. They headed north hand-in-hand, crossing St. Clair Avenue and walking up the long grassy slope of Mall B above the underground Convention Center until they got to the end which overlooked Lakeside Avenue. Jamal leaned on the clear retaining wall and searched to the east.

"There." The Baron pointed at a woman coming down the steps of City Hall. She turned their way. "There she is."

Amy watched the woman walk towards them. "Who's she?"

"Oh…just a bit of entertainment I've arranged for our law enforcement friends." Jamal scanned the sidewalk back behind the woman. "She works in the City Planning Department. Now, that's ironic, given our conversation just a moment ago, no?"

"Are you going to—"

"And there. Yes, there is our helpful friend for the evening." He pointed to a man following behind the woman. "He comes to us from a biowaste disposal company which services local hospitals. Again, ironic."

"Please don't."

The Baron smiled at Amy, then tracked the woman as she passed by on the sidewalk below. A short time later, her preprogrammed synthoid predator passed by, closing the gap bit-by-bit."

"Shall we?" Jamal asked Amy.

"I don't want to see. *Please.*"

"Oh, no. Nothing like that."

"Then what are we going to do?"

Jamal thought for a moment. "We're going to make a little splash of our own."

They went back down Mall B to St. Clair, then walked west into the Warehouse District. They crossed West 6th Street and went to the corner at Lakeside to wait.

The rush of homeward bound workers had slowed back down to a trickle when caretaker Bill pulled up to the corner in the black SUV. Waitress Amy got out of the back, her wrist held tight in the hydraulic clutch of a synthoid.

"Let me go! Let me go! Let me—" she cried out before the Baron muffled her plea by grabbing her mouth hard with his hand.

Orphan Amy noticed a few pedestrians look their way. They all kept on walking.

Jamal shook his head in disgust at waitress Amy until she submitted. He released her and pointed up the West 6th Street exit ramp off the Shoreway.

The synthoid dragged waitress Amy out into the middle of the street and began walking up the ramp.

"Stay by me," Jamal said to orphan Amy as he followed close behind the synthoid, who calmly waved its free hand at the oncoming traffic.

Cars skidded and sideswiped one another as they careened to avoid hitting the four crazy-drunk pedestrians heading upstream.

Jamal smiled when he heard the cry of sirens rise up nearby. Soon after, one last car drifted past. The driver honked and shook a fist at them in anger.

The four walked to the center of the span of the now empty Main Avenue Bridge and waited.

***~~~***

# The River Styx

By the time Maddie arrived with Wally and Jake arrived with Derek, the span of the Main Avenue Bridge had been cleared of wrecks with patrol cars blocking off each end. They met EC at the SWAT tactical van parked at the top of the Lakeside Avenue exit ramp off the Shoreway next to the Archer Apartment building.

"He's been asking for you two," Sergeant Kovacic said, pointing at Maddie and Jake when they got to the back of the van.

"Yeah. No surprise there," Jake said. "What's the situation?"

"We've got snipers up on the Ernst and Young Tower and up on the roof here. Not the best, but workable. There are two perps. One has a child with a gun to her head. The lunatic is sitting on the south wall a hundred feet up."

"Where's the girl," Maddie asked.

"Standing between his legs. We've got a clear shot, but it looks like they're cuffed together at the wrists—which kind of limits our options." Kovacic zoomed in the camera view from the sniper's nest on his *iSlate* to show them. "The other is holding a woman. From the thermals, it looks like that one is a droid. They're out a quarter-mile over the river."

Maddie drew her Glock. "Shall we?"

Jake unholstered his Smith and Wesson *eM&P* to take down the synthoid. It whined as he cycled the charging sequence. He looked at Wally and Derek. "You guys in?"

"Got your back," Wally said, pulling out his pistol.

Derek drew his weapon, too.

EC unshouldered his shotgun.

The five started walking west into the twilight, spreading out across the three traffic lanes as they went with Jake and Maddie out front slightly.

"Jamal!" Jake called out as they got near. He signaled for Wally and Derek to hang back. To EC on his right, he whispered, "Wait, and when we get up there, hop the median and get on the other side of them."

"Hello, Jake, my old friend," the Baron said loudly. "So glad you could make it."

"Can Maddie and I come up there?"

"Sure. *Come on down.*"

Maddie and Jake hugged the concrete median wall, keeping as much distance as possible between them and the Baron on the south side of the roadway. EC climbed over the wall and used it for cover to move to the west of the group. Wally and Derek inched a bit closer on the east flank, their weapons at the ready.

Orphan Amy felt the handcuff come off her wrist, but Jamal held her tight by the collar of her dress. She felt the press of his pistol on her shoulder again.

The synthoid held waitress Amy in front like a shield with a firm grip on each of her biceps.

"Jake, help me," waitress Amy screamed in panic. "Please, help me."

"Shut up!" Jamal yelled angrily at her.

The synthoid shook her into silence.

"It does appear we've got a, mmm, whaddaya call, a

situation, here," Jake said with a big smile, his *eM&P* discreetly aimed at the synthoid from the hip.

"Yeah. Look at us. One big happy family of man out here together," Jamal answered, his baritone voice calm and smooth again. "It is a beautiful evening. You missed a gorgeous sunset."

Maddie held Jamal in the sites of her Glock. She noticed orphan Amy's new dress and the makeup that gave her a more mature beauty.

"I have to admit, you've got a great view here," said Jake. "The lake. The city. You've got it all."

"So, what should we talk about?" asked Jamal. "The weather, perhaps."

"We don't need to talk," Jake said. "There's nothing to discuss, really. Is there?"

"You want to know why, though, right?"

"Nah. I know evil when I see it," Jake dismissed. "I don't need to read a manifesto or hear a speech. They're usually pretty boring anyway. And in the end…it's just evil."

"Quite the moralist, are we?"

"Maybe we could talk about how—like how you want this to end, but I think I know that, too. You're not really much of a man of mystery, Jamal. Or should I call you *Enoch?*"

"So, you know it all, do you?"

"No. I don't know where that crazy brain experiment you had down in the Flats went, but I'm sure it'll turn up again. Right?"

"It is block-chained everywhere. You'll never root it all out."

Jake laughed. "I guess that means job security for me and EC, no?"

"Do not mock me." There was a harsh growl in the Baron's voice.

Jake stared Jamal down.

"*Jake…*" Maddie whispered.

"This whole scene is a mockery," Jake said, waving his pistol. "Like a bad 'B' movie."

"I deserve respect."

Jake rubbed his chin with his left hand. "No…I don't think so."

"And I…will…have it." Jamal raised his voice and looked up to the stars as he cried out, *"Father!"*

Jake caught a slight movement in the triggered synthoid. He raised his *eM&P*.

"Jake, no," Maddie pleaded.

Jake fired, but the electro-magnetic pulse only weakened the synthoid. It still effortlessly tossed waitress Amy over its shoulder and off the bridge like a rag doll.

As the scream faded in the hundred-foot fall to the water, orphan Amy felt Jamal release his grip on her collar. She instinctively ran towards Maddie.

Maddie fired ten rounds from her Glock. The forty-caliber slugs slammed into Jamal's chest pushing him back and over the south wall. She grabbed Amy in a hug and turned, putting her body between the girl and the synthoid.

The Baron fell in silence.

Jake dropped the synthoid into a twitching spasm on the road bed with a second EMP round.

A faint splash was heard from below.

***~~~***

# A Beautiful Friendship

Q sat in a chair on the visitor's side of his own desk next to Jake, watching Lt. Sands on the other side oversee the city IT technician scrubbing Q's desktop, laptop, and *iSlate*, deleting his log-in IDs and wiping his data files. Two uniformed officers stood outside his office on either side of the door.

"Are you sure you don't want your union rep here?" Lt. Sands asked. "I think I'd feel better about this if he was."

"Nah, I'm good with Jake," Q said. "I trust him."

"And why not?" Jake asked with a touch of bitterness. "I shot a Councilman's son dead and I've still got my badge."

"That is not funny, mister." Sands shot his finger across the desk at Jake.

"Yes, sir."

"And don't call me sir."

"Yes, sir."

"Damn it." Sands pointed at Q. "Such misplaced trust was probably your first mistake."

"Sadly, no. Just the latest in a long, long chain of errors and miscalculations," Q said. "And, it likely won't be my last."

Lt. Sands shook his head and turned back to observe the IT Tech.

"You know," Q said to Jake, "I was up on the roof at White Chapel that night."

"Oh, yeah?"

"Yeah. I saw the Baron fall."

*"Really."*

Lt. Sands crossed his arms against his chest and pinched his eyes shut, trying hard to ignore their banter.

"Man, he pancaked into the river good," Q said. "Real good."

"That Maddie…she's a hell of a shot."

"Couldn't have happened to a nicer guy."

"Yeah, it could have," Jake said. "But I'm glad it didn't."

"All done," said the IT tech. "I just need his phone and *iNode.*"

Q pointed to the credenza behind his desk, where a single cell phone was neatly placed next to his *iNode.*

"Just one?" Sands asked, then changed his mind. "No-no-no, I don't want to know."

The IT tech scooped them up. Sands, Jake, and Q watched him leave.

"Finally, I need your passkey, dongle and department ID." Sands held out his hand.

Q took off the lanyard with the requested items from around his neck and dropped it into the Lieutenant's hand.

Lt. Sands pulled a letter from his leather portfolio. "Here is your official notice of suspension—with pay, for now. You will get notification of the date and time of the administrative hearing by certified mail."

Q took the letter. The smile fell from his face.

"I'm sorry about all this, but…"

"It's okay. I'm the one who screwed the pooch," Q said.

Lt. Sands sighed. "Anyway, I need to get down to Public

Square for a meeting with the Director and you have to be escorted from the building."

"I want to collect my pictures and some personal items." Q pointed to the Mondrian and Warhol prints on the office wall. "Can Jake walk me out?"

"Yeah, I can take care of that, Lieu," Jake said.

Lt. Sands looked at Q, then Jake. "All right. But the uniforms stay."

Q and Jake nodded like scolded school boys.

The Lieutenant stepped out, spoke with the uniformed officers, then left the building. The patrolmen turned to watch Q and Jake through the glass front wall of the office.

"It's not his fault," Jake said to Q. "Sands is just an errand boy for the Captain, who's in overdrive CYA mode. You know management."

Q shrugged. "What is it you always say about the Captain?"

Jake chuckled. "I'm only six numbers away from telling that guy what I really think of him."

"Yeah, well, now we're only three…maybe even two." A smile slowly grew on Q's face.

Jake looked over and cocked his head.

Q exaggerated his lip movements as he silently formed the words, *Four…Hundred…Fifty…Million…Dollars…*

"Courtesy of esquires Howard, Fine and Howard?"

"Stooges by any other name are still stooges."

"You found it?"

"I'm close." Q gave Jake a conspiratorial wink. "I'm just surprised there wasn't a bigger uproar when it went missing."

"I'm not. Something about that whole deal always gave me pause." Jake frowned. "Wait a minute…*We?*"

"I'm selfish, but I'm not greedy," Q said. "Besides, I might need a helping hand along the way."

"Louie, I think this is the beginning of a beautiful friendship." Jake grabbed Q's shoulder and squeezed.

"Who's Louie?" Q asked.

"Who cares. Let's get your stuff and blow this pop stand."

***~~***

# Maddie and Jake

"I'm sorry, Jake." Maddie reached across the booth and took his hand. She squeezed.

"Yeah, I figured. Why didn't you say something?"

"Frankly, I knew you would talk me out of it." Maddie sighed. "So, I waited until I interviewed and made up my mind for sure."

"Can't talk you out of it?"

"Too late now."

"Why?"

"I need to break the cycle. With everything that's happened…" Maddie looked away. She scanned the deli dining room. "You'll be fine."

"I really don't think I will be fine." Jake smiled. "But I'm happy for you. Quantico. A fed, huh?"

Maddie nodded.

"And here I took you at your word, you'd be going back to Robbery/Homicide."

"When the Bureau came to town after, Sands and the Captain played me up, and…well, the suits bought it. They must be desperate to staff the new unit with experienced people."

Jake took a sip of coffee.

"It really should have been you, though."

"No. I get it. Too much baggage." He shook his head. "And I was never the Captain's favorite. You hungry?"

"No, really. I've got to get going. A million-and-one things to tend to before the move."

"What about Amy?"

"She's doing very well. She's with folks in Westlake—real close to me. I've seen her a few times. She seems happy."

"And when you leave?"

"She's a tough cookie."

"Like you?"

"Tougher, I think. She'll be fine." Maddie stood up. "We'll talk, okay?"

Jake nodded. He looked up from his mug. "I love you, Mads."

"Oh, Jake…I—I—" Maddie leaned over and kissed the top of Jake's head.

"Take good care. *Please.*"

Maddie smiled, turned and walked away. She stopped at the register and wiped a tear away. "Uncle Cutty…"

Cutty set down his butcher knife, took off his apron and came out from behind the meat counter. He gave her a big hug. "We'll all miss you, Missy *Mad-de-line.*"

Maddie sniffed. She looked back over Cutty's shoulder at Jake.

Jake waved.

*I should have told him…* Maddie buried her face in Cutty's shoulder. *But no…I'll wait a few months, when I'm starting to show.*

***~~~***

# Home

Amy left her suburban foster home in Westlake at the regular time for school but went to Crocker Park instead. She boarded the RTA Cleveland State Line bus with the morning commuters headed downtown for work. She stared blankly out the window at the passing shops, restaurants, office buildings, and strip malls on Detroit Avenue, then at the big houses of rich people lining Clifton Boulevard.

Forty minutes later, she got off at the West 117th Street stop. It was a longer walk from there, but the bus would continue down the Shoreway and over the Main Avenue Bridge. Amy just could not bear returning to that place above the river again.

Amy walked south to the Rapid Transit station and took the next eastbound train to West 65th Street. She walked north to Franklin Avenue, then turned towards downtown until she got to West 44th Street.

"Welcome home, child," Stephanie said when she answered Amy's knock at the front door. "What took you so long?"

***~~~***

*Thank you for reading my story.*

## About M.T. Bass

M.T. Bass lives, writes, flies, and plays music in Mudcat Falls, USA.

www.MTBass.net

## Available in Paperback & eBook

Artificial Intelligence? *Fuhgeddaboudit!*

Artificial Evil has a name…*Munchausen.*

When androids are reprogrammed into hit men, detectives of the Artificial Crimes Unit repo the AnSub and track down the hackers. Partners Jake and EC's case of an "extra-judicial" divorce settlement takes a nasty turn with DNA from a hundred-year-old murder in Boston and a signature that harkens back to the very first serial killer ever in London.

www.MTBass.net

The Darknet
Murder by Munchausen #2
A NOVEL BY M.T. BASS

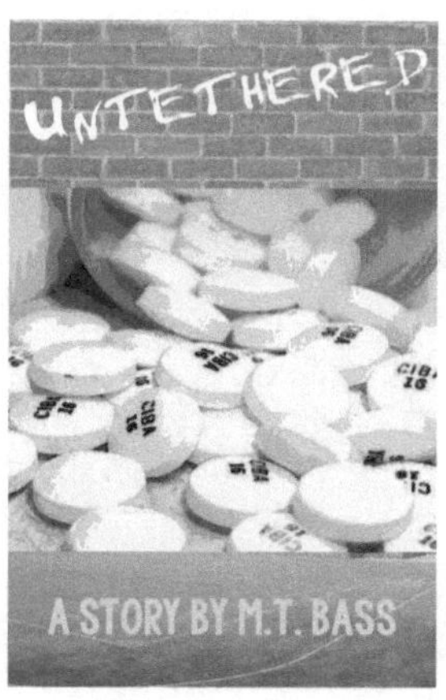


## Available in eBook

At District High School #6241, Connor wants only to get close to Liz, the cheerleader whose locker is just across the hall, and forget the suicide of his father in jail, but his family's dark past and a rebellious nature force him to the fringes of student social circles and into an unlikely alliance to fight back against a tyranny of conformity.

www.MTBass.net

## Available in Paperback & eBook

People ask me where I get the ideas for my books. In this case, I recall reading about Alaska bush pilots for fun. I must have watched *Animal House* and *Treasure of the Sierra Madre* around that time and…a few months later—Eureka! The words for the prologue and first chapter just started spilling out of my head. ("Clean up on aisle five.")

Seriously, what could go wrong? *Love & Betrayal…Murder & Mayhem…Friendship & Double-Crossing Partners in Pursuit of Buried Treasure…*

www.MTBass.net

## Available in eBook

*Lodging — bending of the stalk of a plant (stalk lodging)
or the entire plant (root lodging)*

While World War II engulfs every nation on the globe, Rebecca and her high school friend Sarah can only dream of escaping a dreary, wind-blown existence in western Kansas, until their boring, stodgy old hometown fills with handsome young men learning to fly Army Air Corps bombers known as *Liberators*, and their lives are suddenly filled with temptation and, perhaps, true love.

www.MTBass.net

## Available in Paperback & eBook

Kansas City, 1965 — Y.T. Erp, Jr. can't wait to leave for college at the University of California, Berkeley to escape not only the work, but especially all the phlegm-brained idiots at his father's aerospace company.  Leaving behind a pregnant auburn-haired cheerleader, a sensuous red-headed siren plotting to usurp his familial ties, and his two best friends—one who ends up in Vietnam and the other in the Weather Underground—his "trip" on the wild side of the Generation Gap takes him from the psychedelic scene of Haight-Ashbury to the F.B.I.'s Ten Most Wanted list.  Meanwhile, his father is consumed by the task of managing his unmanageable corporate team in the quest to help fulfill a President's challenge to "land a man on the moon."

www.MTBass.net

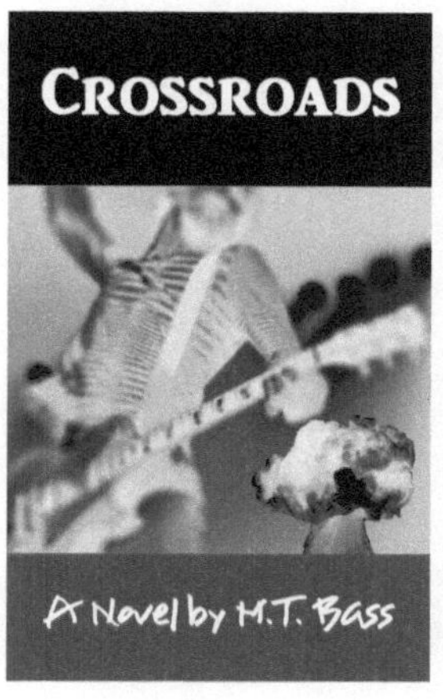


## Available in eBook

Cleveland, 1977 — Grappling with a foreign policy crisis, the U.S. Government targets a hapless rock-'n'-roller as a Russian spy in a classic case of mistaken identity for an innocent, 'Wrong Man' hero…or *is he?*

Think of an unholy fictional union between the Rolling Stones and Alfred Hitchcock's *North by Northwest.*

Unlike any novel you have ever read, this one has a soundtrack. After all, a story whose characters are musicians should have…well…*music.* Right?

www.MTBass.net

## Available in Paperback & eBook

Hollywood, 1950 — Former P-51 fighter pilot A. Gavin Byrd is on location for a movie shoot, when he gets a call from the police that his older brother, a prominent Beverly Hills plastic surgeon, has been found dead on his boat. The Lieutenant in charge of the investigation is ready to close the case as a suicide from the start, but "Hawk" doesn't buy it and decides to find out what really happened for himself.

With help from a former starlet ex-girlfriend, a friendly police sergeant whose life was saved in the war by his brother and a nosy Los Angeles Times reporter, Hawk's search for the truth takes him through cross-fire, dog fights and mine fields in Hollywood, Beverly Hills, Burbank and Las Vegas, and leads him into some of the darker corners of his brother's patient files and private life that he never knew existed.

www.MTBass.net

www.ingramcontent.com/pod-product-compliance
Lightning Source LLC
Chambersburg PA
CBHW060556190726
48283CB00003B/1040